Ann Girdharry was born and educated in the UK. A trained psychotherapist, she has worked for many years as a manager in the not-for-profit sector, for agencies working with: carers, vulnerable older people and those with dementia, survivors of abuse, and victims of racism and racial attacks. Today, she lives in Montpellier, France with her husband and two children.

You can find out more about Ann Girdharry by visiting her website – www.girdharry.com

Or catch up with her on social media –

www.goodreads.com/AnnGirdharry
www.bookbub.com/profile/ann-girdharry
www.facebook.com/AnnGirdharryAuthor/

Titles by this author

Kal Medi series

Good Girl Bad Girl
London Noir
The Beauty Killers

Chilling Tales of the Unexpected
Boxed Set

London Noir

Ann Girdharry

For my sister Karen,
who forged good fortune against the odds
and found her own, well-deserved happiness
xx

Chapter One

At Lilac Mansions

Sophie dipped her brush in water and chose sky blue to finish the detail.

The colour reminded her of summer days. It also reminded Sophie of her mother, and, as usual, that brought a bitter taste to the back of her mouth. Sophie swallowed. Concentrating to stop the trembling in her fingers, with two strokes, she finished the butterfly wings. The makeup brush clattered onto the dresser. Sophie twisted towards the mirror and admired the trail of tiny, blue butterflies sweeping over her shoulder.

Her clutch bag was on the bed and she placed inside it the syringe, loaded and ready for its victim. Then she picked up the perfume and pepper spray, the jasmine scent sickly sweet. The spray was a noxious mix, designed to blind the victim and even better, make them writhe in agony. That's why Lady Penny made sure all the girls carried it.

Last, Sophie took the flick knife and touched her finger to the razor-sharp edge. Sugar G trained them – a strike to the eye, to the crease of the groin, or the stomach – all the soft parts of the body. Not all the girls carried a knife, and she was sure of those who did, none of them carried it to commit murder.

Chapter Two

Smack-smack. Smack-smack. The wipers struggled with the downpour.

Kal swore to herself. 'It's supposed to be summer, not a bloody monsoon.'

As she swerved to avoid a puddle as big as a pond, an oncoming driver blared his horn.

'Get out of my way, moron,' Kal shouted.

She thumped the steering wheel twice before she got a grip.

Hey, calm down, this isn't going to get you to the hospital any faster.

For the past four months, she couldn't get the machines out of her mind. Those blinking, bleeping machines were imprinted on the inside of her eyelids. The real machinery sat alongside Marty's bed monitoring her heart rate and arterial oxygen levels.

Kal visited the hospital three times a week and hadn't let herself slack off. It was a question of loyalty and missing even a single visit would've been like admitting what a bad friend she was. That she'd given up on Marty and left her. Again. Which was out of the question.

Another driver blared their horn and she jolted back to the present. Ever since the text message from Marty's brother, her pulse was racing. Marty was out of the coma. She was awake. And downpour or not, Kal had to get there.

At the next intersection with the traffic lights on green, Kal took the corner at speed.

'No!'

She slammed on the brakes and the car skidded.

There was no traction under the tyres, only slewing water. Time slowed and the back of the car swung in an arc. She tried to keep sight of the small, dark figure in her path and every muscle tensed. A soft *thump* against the bumper would mean disaster.

When the car slammed into the kerbside, it ricocheted her head off the headrest, the seatbelt tight across her chest. Kal stared out at the downpour. She had to kick herself into action and prise her own fingers from the steering wheel. Her own panting was horribly loud as she fumbled for the door latch.

Rain poured down. Caught in the headlights, a figure hunched at the roadside. It was a young girl. She was right at the edge of the pavement.

Please, please let her be okay.

'Hey – are you all right?'

Rain was pouring down Kal's neck.

'Did I hit you?'

With no jacket and with blonde hair plastered to her head, the girl kept her face low and buried in a red scarf. A sudden instinct stopped Kal from reaching out. She straightened up and wiped the water from her eyes.

'Are you all right?' She asked in a gentler voice.

It took a few seconds for the girl to respond. It seemed like hours.

The girl nodded.

'I'm so sorry.'

Kal kept still, standing in water deep enough to flow over her shoes. Something was wrong. This wasn't a child, the girl looked like a teenager, maybe older. If she wasn't hurt, why hadn't she started talking? Why was she still cowering?

'I lost control of the car. Can I help you?'

The girl gave a quick glance up, her gaze not making it to Kal's eyes.

'Did I give you a fright?' Kal said.

The girl nodded.

'I'm really sorry.'

'I didn't look where I was going.' She sounded as frail as she looked.

Kal thought back –the figure had dashed out at the last minute. The girl must have been running.

'I'm the one to blame. In weather like this I should've been extra careful,' Kal said.

The girl uncurled a little and rubbed the scarf across her nose. Kal shelved her relief. There was something wrong here, if not from an injury then from what?

'My name's Kal.'

The girl's eyes darted from side to side. Her arms were wrapped across her chest.

'Hey we're getting soaked, please let me offer you a ride.'

Was she in shock? Was she on drugs? The way the girl eyed Kal said she'd refuse any offer of help. But it made Kal even more determined to find a way to reach out because it was pretty obvious this girl was in trouble.

'What do you say? Shall we get out of this downpour?'

She realised she'd left the driver's door wide open. Shit, the girl hadn't been the only one terrified. Kal reached behind to open the passenger door and gave a nod and a smile of encouragement. This was the moment of truth, when the girl could do a runner.

She knew she couldn't force someone to accept help, but her psychological training meant she could read this girl. Something had terrified her and Kal wasn't convinced it was the near-miss.

Rain splattered on the roof.

They both saw the lights of the other car at the same time. It cruised towards the intersection and the girl jerked upright as if someone jabbed her with an electric rod. She dived behind Kal and into the back seat. Kal slammed the door behind her.

When Kal got in the front, the upholstery squelched. It smelled of wet clothes and wet hair.

'So where are you headed?' Kal asked, making no comment about how her passenger had ducked down out of sight. As the oncoming car cruised across the junction, Kal clocked its details.

The girl sat up slowly. She had a pale complexion and delicate, elfin looks. There were no visible bruises or marks, and she didn't appear homeless because she wore expensive clothing. Better not to ask for the girl's name because it would come over as pressure.

In the rear-view mirror, attractive, almond-shaped eyes met Kal's gaze.

'Something tells me you're in a rush to get somewhere too,' the girl said.

'How'd you work that out?'

'From the look on your face, and people don't dash around in weather like this unless they have to.'

That was a surprise. So, she was petrified and running and yet she had a grasp on analysing other people.

'You're right,' Kal said, 'I need to get to the hospital.'

'What for?'

'To see my best friend.'

'A 'she' or a 'he'?'

'A 'she' and her name's Marty.'

'I guess she's ill then?'

'There was a terrible accident and Marty's been in a coma. Her brother just contacted me to say she's conscious. I know there's no excuse for it but that's why I was rushing when I shouldn't have been.'

Keeping the girl talking would be the best way to build a bridge. She hoped it would give her a chance of finding out more. She'd promised herself she'd use her father's training for the good, and here was an opportunity.

'Marty's family are there so I might not get any time with her, but I was so grateful when I got the message.'

She pulled away from the kerb. 'I've been desperate. I kept wishing it was me on that bed and it's been driving me crazy. I was the worst type of friend Marty could have.' Kal clamped her mouth shut. She wouldn't normally spill out to a stranger, or to anyone for that matter.

'Yeah, I understand. When you love someone, everything gets twisted out of line.'

In the mirror, those almond eyes met Kal's again and her assessment of the girl shifted. This girl had found a way through Kal's armour as if it were the easiest thing in the world. And that was far from true – Kal could count the people she trusted with her feelings on less than one hand.

'Marty's accident wasn't your fault.'

Actually, it was, thought Kal.

In an instant she was back there. Surrounded by the stinking sewers. Swimming for her life through pitch-black tunnels. At night, she still jerked awake to the feeling of icy water creeping up her body, ready to drown her screams. In the sewers, Kal had discovered who her father really was and what he had done, and it had taken her to hell and back. And whilst they'd held her prisoner, the Syndicate had been closing in on the people she loved. Marty had been alone and all Marty's kung fu expertise hadn't been enough to save her. Yes, Kal blamed herself. For failing to protect her friends.

She gritted her teeth.

'We always blame ourselves for stuff we've no control over, that's what I think,' the girl said. 'So you should let yourself off the hook.'

8

Kal concentrated on the road. The girl was spot on with her comments and that was spooky, especially for someone so young. Kal knew you only got that type of insight in special circumstances, like if you were brainwashed from an early age by an expert in psychology, as Kal had been by her criminal father. Or, if you learned to analyse other people because you felt it was the only way of keeping yourself alive. Yes, survival, that's what her intuition was telling her – this girl had been in a life or death situation.

'Where can I take you? You didn't say yet.'

'We're going in the right direction, so I didn't need to. I'm heading for Montgomery Road. D'you know it?'

Kal hid her reaction. Everyone around here knew Montgomery. It was the red-light district of this part of London, full of drug addicts and underage prostitutes and definitely not the place for a vulnerable young woman. This was going from bad to worse.

'I think so. Do you have friends there? Family?'

If she asked too many questions, the girl would clam up. Montgomery was only a couple of streets away, so Kal took a wrong turn down a one-way system.

'If you must know, I've a friend there.'

'Someone you can trust?'

'Since when is a friend someone you can't trust?'

Kal let the wipers do a couple of sweeps before she spoke again.

'I guess you know it's a red-light area. It doesn't feel right dropping you there and it's going to be night soon.

Why not stay at my place? No questions asked I promise, and you can head off in the morning.'

'You said you'd drop me where I wanted. You think I'm some kind of dumb-ass who doesn't know how to look after myself? Of course I know it's where the prostitutes hang out.'

'Listen if you're in trouble, I can help.'

'I don't need your help! Let me out.' The girl yanked at the door handle.

Shit. Kal pulled over and twisted around.

'Please don't run off. I respect your choices and your life is your business. I only want to make sure you're safe.'

She clicked off the central locking and though the girl kept hold of the handle, she didn't pull at it again.

'I know you mean it in a good way.' The girl sniffed. 'But don't behave like an idiot.'

'You seem like a nice kid and, believe me, that's not something I say often. If you won't take up my offer then at least let me take you to the door. Please?'

'O...kay. Number thirty-three. And don't turn down that stupid one-way system again.'

They arrived in Montgomery Road far too soon. Three-storey terraced houses ran the length of the street. With red brick walls and Georgian bay windows they were all the same and the eye was caught by a long row of front doors, each painted a different colour. The door to number thirty-three was bright red.

'Look, I don't want to be out-of-line but I'd really like to help. If you're in some sort of trouble...'

'I'm really not. I'll be totally okay.'

Kal pulled on the hand brake. 'Be safe. I tell you what, why don't I give you my number in case?'

'Go to your friend, she'll be glad to see you…'

'I'm not so sure about that.'

'…oh, and I didn't tell you, my name's Sophie.'

'I'm sorry again about earlier Sophie, and if you ever need–'

Sophie didn't stop to hear the rest. She was already out of the car and running towards the red door. Kal watched Sophie standing in the rain, watched her ring the bell, and then watched her disappear inside.

Chapter Three

I suppose the realisation I was different stole up on me slowly.

There were signs from early on if I'm honest. Like my first year in primary school when Mirabella wet her knickers in front of the whole class – the girls were mortified and the boys laughed and I was excited.

So yeah, I knew I was different. To survive, I learned to act like my friends and I'm so good, pretty much everyone in my life would say I'm normal. I like it because it means I'm clever.

One thing I've learned is that when you've wanted something for a long time, your mind makes tracks in the sand showing exactly how it's going to turn out. You anticipate your own reactions, and what the other person will say and do. Those tracks start out delicate and then solidify with each replaying of the fantasy, until they get to be as firm as a rail track.

The fantasy can keep me occupied for months. After it's run its course, the enacting is the real deal. I have to have it – the flash of horror in their eyes, the desperate urge to plea for mercy, bowels voiding and dribbling down a leg. It's the helplessness which grabs me – when they realise there's absolutely nothing they can do. It's the most exhilarating drug in the world.

For me, it's the eyes that are captivating. The windows of the soul – unable to lie in the final moments.

Chapter Four

When Marty awoke, it seemed as if moments before she'd been fighting for her life down a London alley. She remembered being alone, and at the end, how scared she'd been. With four highly-trained assailants against her, the odds were stacked the wrong way.

They'd overwhelmed her, despite her kung fu skills and her strength and agility which made her so good in the combat room. In the end they beat her down until nothing was left but her will to live. Then, even that had poured out, along with her blood, into the gutter. It was a miracle she'd survived and she'd take that miracle any day. So it was a surprise to wake up and stare at a white ceiling and listen to the calm voices of strangers.

Part of Marty recalled her mother's prayers drifting through from far away, and the presence of her mother at her bedside, although she wondered if that was a dream, taken from her childhood and fashioned into the here and now. Anyway, it wasn't long after she awoke that her mother arrived. Of course, her mother cried. Even her hard-nosed brother, Vince, cried. Marty lay there talking a few words and preventing herself from falling into an exhausted daze, waiting for the arrival of her best friend.

This would be tricky. Marty knew if she played it wrong she might lose Kal forever.

They'd been friends since primary school and it was their friendship which had kept both of them going, kept both of them focusing ahead and on getting away from their difficult childhoods. Away from their fathers, both twisted and abusive in their own ways. Though Kal never saw it like that, because Kal's father had tutored his daughter and taught her everything he knew and crafted her to be like him.

Yes, this would be complicated. Kal would've been brought to her knees by guilt. She would've fixed on things she should have done differently rather than focusing on what she'd done right and who she'd saved and that's where Marty came in. She must find a way of putting Kal back on track.

Marty waited until the nurse announced a final visitor.

When Kal knocked twice, Marty's stomach began to ache. This might be worse than she thought – the Kal Marty knew would've barged straight in.

'Hey, long time no see. You're looking good, Marty.'

'Like hell I am.'

Kal laughed and Marty heard the same small choking sound she'd heard at the back of her brother's throat.

'Oh no, don't tell me I'm knocked out for a few days and you start cracking up. Give me a break.'

'It was months, Marty. They smashed you up so bad the doctors hardly saved you and we didn't know if you'd revive and if you did…'

'…if I did, whether I'd be a vegetable? No news on that one, ha,ha, though I'll be having tests that'll assess pretty much every poor cell in my body. And what the hell happened to you? You took a shower with your clothes on?'

'I ran into some trouble on the way here,' Kal said. 'Tell you about it another time.'

Marty tried not to cough and failed. Even to her own ears, it was a weak, horrible cough. The kind you'd expect from a sickly, old person and Marty had already seen the horror on her mother's face in response to it. Now she watched as Kal clenched her jaw.

'For goodness sake, just let it out will you? Of course Mum did, and even my brother did, so you might as well get it over with. A bit of blubbering never hurt anyone.'

'I'm sorry and god, that sounds so inadequate I feel like punching myself in the head. I've been over what I wanted to say a million times and it never sounded right. It was my fault. It was my fault you were in that alley. I wish it had been me and not you.'

'It's okay, I'm back now, and Kal, I'm so sorry. It sounds like hell. Mum told me what happened.'

'You're not the one who should be sorry. Look what I did to *you*.'

Marty half-closed her eyes and listened to the steady beeping of a monitoring machine. Yup, Kal had dug herself into one deep hole and built those walls up around herself like she liked to do, thick and solid.

'I thought you'd be mad at me,' Kal said.

Marty took a deep breath. 'I *am* mad at you, for being such an idiot to think you decide what *I* do. I made my decision to stick with it to the end. I knew the risks, so you can forget any guilt tripping.' Marty felt her strength draining away. 'You nailed him, didn't you? That sick bastard.'

'Yes,' said Kal in a low voice.

'It's all that matters. And you don't even realise, but you're the only one who could've done it. *You* tracked him, *you* manoeuvred yourself into the right place at the right time and *you* waited for the moment to bring him down. You can do things other people can't. All that stuff your father forced into you wasn't a curse because you've got talents and skills other people dream of. Me being in the alley meant you were left free and I don't regret a thing.'

The machines bleeped and Marty rested back on the pillow, short of breath.

'You wouldn't believe the fatigue – they say it's muscle wastage. I can hardly lift my own damn head.'

The choking sound in Kal's throat was much louder.

Marty kept her eyes closed. She felt herself phasing out, then remembered there was something else she wanted to say. 'Yeah, and with everyone acting so nervous and scared of you, without me around to kick your butt into line, who's there to do it?'

'Oh Marty. What would I do without you?'

There was a pause and then Kal started sobbing. Job done, Marty thought, and she let the tiredness wash over her.

Chapter Five

Kal tossed a ball of tissues in the bin. On her way past, she said goodbye to the nurses at the desk. They both gave her an odd look. Gosh, thought Kal, she must have been doing a lot of scowling at them these last few months. What had they been calling her behind her back? Anti-social? Scary? Or simply, strange? Kal had been called plenty of names in her time and she supposed if she'd had a normal childhood she wouldn't come across so badly. But her father, David Khan, had been in the employ of the Cartel. He'd been a top-level criminal – surveillance, subterfuge, gathering of high class, counter-intelligence, and like Marty always said, his aim was for Kal to be just like him.

Outside in the fresh air, she headed across the car park. Time to go back for Sophie. Kal hadn't been making it up when she said Sophie was a nice kid and she was pretty certain the girl was being chased. Or hunted. Or stalked. And no way was she leaving Sophie to deal with that on her own. Zipping up her jacket, Kal strode back to her car.

***

Back at number thirty-three, dusk was settling in. Montgomery Road lay quiet, except for a posse of women loitering near the end of the street. Luckily for the prostitutes, the rain clouds had cleared. The street smelled newly-washed fresh and clean. Accumulated debris had been swept down the drains and the long line of parked cars glistened.

Kal walked over to the group. There were eight women in all and they were talking to a man. Or rather, a man was talking to them. He looked out of place in his classy jacket and expensive shoes.

She remembered the sound of her father's voice in her earpiece.

"Go talk to the woman at the counter and find out what type of person she is."

"Ask that officer for help and find her weaknesses."

David Khan would analyse the information Kal gathered. Under his strict guidance, she learned to track and interpret the smallest details in the people they observed. She learned how to analyse the make-up of each target and how to apply her knowledge to slip in unseen and unnoticed.

They gained entry to private functions, they infiltrated secure rooms at a bank, at a major police station, and at a millionaire's mansion. All using subterfuge. All by tricking ordinary people using psychological strategy, and only force when absolutely necessary.

"Use your knowledge. Reflect back to people exactly what they want to see and hear. Be the person they expect. Like that you won't ruffle any feathers and the power is yours," her father said.

Kal took a calming breath and let the flashback fade. She hoped one day all the bad memories of him would be washed away.

She made sure to approach out of the group's line of sight. This was possible with everyone except the man. She kept her head down. With their interest focused on him, none of the women paid Kal any attention.

'Please pass it around and I'll give a reward to anyone who has information,' the man said, pushing a flyer towards the women.

At the edge of the huddle, she kept still, careful not to make any waves. Kal glanced at the paper the man held out and her senses snapped to alert. The girl in the picture was blonde and her hair blew in the breeze and there was no mistaking – it was Sophie.

Who was he? What was going on here? She must find out quickly. And pick up all the nuances and the subtext and everything that was said and left unsaid.

With sandy hair and hazel eyes, the man was tall and not bad looking. He had an awkwardness in the way he held himself, as if he felt permanently ill-at-ease. His smart jacket was unbuttoned to show an equally expensive shirt. Kal wondered if he spent money in his appearance to divert from his discomfort around others. Smooth skin, good complexion, well groomed – Kal saw no trace of Sophie in his features.

The women were a closed-mouth crew. It would be part of their tactics – never give details to punters, don't talk about the other prostitutes, don't let slip any personal information, keep the ring tight. Nobody broke the code because it kept them safe.

'Has anyone seen her? It's important.'

One of the women placed a painted nail on Sophie's face. 'She's pretty. Did she run out on you? What a shame.'

They were teasing him.

'Are you mad at her, honey?' asked another woman, her voice full of mockery.

The man was struggling. The power was with the women and they were making the most of it because he presented an easy target. Obviously not a cop, and out of place in this environment. Kal watched his attention flicking from one face to the other as he tried to find a way through the barriers.

'No, dammit, she's my sister.'

'That's what they all say!'

'I know she's been here before. Please take a look at the photograph – she's changed a lot in the last couple of years. Have you seen her recently?'

He thrust the flyer towards the women but none of them would take it. Unconsciously, they had encircled him, completing the scenario of a gaggle of witches ringing their victim.

'It's the truth, she's vulnerable and she needs to be in care. Sophie needs help.'

That word snagged the attention of one of them – a brunette with a purple streak in her hair. Kal watched the brunette shift from one foot to the other, now unable to stop her eyes gravitating to Sophie's picture. The woman with the purple streak must feel an affinity with a girl in need of help. Kal wondered when this woman had needed help herself, and whether she'd ever received it.

'That sounds kinda serious,' said the woman with the purple streak.

'She's a danger to herself because she… she's going through a difficult time. Please, have you seen her?'

Purple-streak hesitated and made to take a flyer. The group quickly gained control. One of them elbowed her out of the way.

'The only thing we're interested in is your money, though you'll get a fair exchange, if you know what I mean.' The woman who said this gave him a wink. 'There's no trade here for information because we've never seen her before.'

They'd won. He'd get nowhere with them, not unless he decided to try sex as a route in. If he chose the woman with the purple hair he might have a chance.

Kal knew he didn't look the type. The man seemed desperate but not enough to push him over a line drawn in his own head that carved out the right side of decent. Kal saw he wouldn't cross it for this girl he called his sister, and the self-imposed limit would mean he'd fail.

He confronted their silence for a few moments more and then turned away. Frustration bowed the top of his back and Kal felt certain he would turn this failure in on himself.

'Come back any time you like, honey. You'll always get a warm welcome,' one of them called after him.

Several of the women laughed.

Kal watched the man walk to his car. It was the same one she'd seen cruise across the junction a few hours before. As he folded his tall frame into the driving seat, Kal thought of Sophie's frailty. Why was this man tailing Sophie? What was he doing here digging for information? Together with her protectiveness towards Sophie, suspicion and anger started mixing in, aimed at this man with the shiny, black shoes.

'He doesn't look like a punter,' said purple-streak.

'Doesn't act like one either and he's not a cop, I can smell cops.'

'You wait and see, in a few weeks he'll be back here for a real trade. That's his way of scouting out the territory.'

'You think? You've been watching too many movies, Candice.'

The women laughed.

'Gosh it's quiet tonight, where are all our usuals? Time to spread out a bit girls. Hey, who the hell are you!'

Kal kept her hands stuffed in her pockets. She could walk away. She could follow the man. Or she could take up the challenge and coax and fashion a way into the middle of this bunch without them even knowing she'd tried. Kal didn't like this man's interest in Sophie and she didn't like that Sophie had disappeared inside a house on this street. No, she was going to get to the bottom of this. Time to get to work.

To win in this situation, she must tuck herself away and study the details of the person in front of her so well, she'd be able to feed them back exactly what they wanted to hear. Yes, to get to Sophie, she'd need to get to the hub of the set-up on Montgomery and get to it fast.

Saying she was a friend of Sophie's was likely to get her thrown onto her backside, literally, because the man had muddied the waters. What she needed was a chance of being an insider. These women must see her as no threat. Needy. An exploitable commodity and a sister to take under their wing. Kal licked her lips. It would be a challenge to pull it off. She'd have to play it just right, but then again, she liked challenges.

'Er, thing is,'

'Speak up, we can't hear you.'

The women laughed and one of them deliberately bumped against Kal's shoulder. Oh yes, Kal thought, I know that game. This could turn into a real bullying session. This was a gang, tightly knit and with a hierarchy. She rubbed her shoulder and pouted.

'What's eating you, sister?' she said.

'I ain't your sister.'

'And I'm not some pussy to be shoved around.'

'Cut her some slack,' Candice said. 'Now what the hell are you doing, nosing around our patch?'

Kal was glad she was wearing a short skirt. It had been a disaster for the thunder storm but now it could be an asset. It had mostly dried out at the hospital, and it clung to her legs, showing plenty of thigh. She'd hitched it up a few inches when she approached the women and it had been a good call. The silk debadeur top wasn't her most alluring – it was a cheap, skimpy number she'd picked up at Camden market and it would have to do. She lifted her chin and gave Candice a level gaze, careful to keep her expression neutral.

'I need the money.'

'You need money?' One of the women said. 'What the fuck are you talking about? We all need money. Now piss off.'

'She's not looking for cash,' said Candice. 'If you walk down this street you only do it for one reason – she wants work, don't you hun?'

Candice wore stiletto-heeled boots, with black leather reaching up to her mid-thighs. Kal rather liked the look of them.

'You're sure as hell not a virgin and you've no experience on the job,' Candice said. 'The only work we can offer you is cleaning the toilets.'

A vicious cackle ran around the group.

Kal stood her ground. 'Like I said, I need the money.'

'Then go and get a job as a waitress and maybe you'll get lucky and shag the owner. Ain't nothing for you here, gal.'

Kal shrugged. 'Fucking the owner is what gave me the problem.'

A couple of the women laughed at the joke, though they kept it subdued.

'You're a funny one, aren't you?' Candice said. She flicked a strand of Kal's jet-black hair, then used her finger to tilt Kal's head to one side, then the other. Kal didn't resist. Now wasn't the time for confrontation.

'Where're you from? India? Sri Lanka?'

'My parents are from India. I was born in London and I grew up here.'

'Lots of men like dark skin like yours and you've a decent body on you but Sugar G doesn't take on newbies, he'll only take a recommendation. Sorry, you'd better run on back home to mummy.'

'I can't do that. This is my last resort. I need the cash and I need it quickly.'

'Fucking hell, you're annoying, aren't you?'

It looked like most of the light had gone out of Candice's eyes a long time ago and the woman gave a cold smile.

Kal made certain to keep out any trace of challenge because she knew, if there was any space for her with these women, it would be at the bottom of the ladder.

She already pegged Candice as the ring leader. Only a person with no home could abandon themselves to this life and only a homeless soul could latch onto Candice as a leader and become part of her tribe. Candice poked her finger hard into Kal's chest. It was a move designed to make Kal take a step back. She didn't.

'There's more spirit kicking around in that head of yours than I thought. What really brought you here?' Candice asked.

Kal watched the woman's heavily mascaraed-eyelids as Candice blinked. She felt a ripple run around the group. Pimps usually had a favourite, and Kal guessed this ringleader, Candice, was top of the list for the man Candice mentioned, Sugar G. The other women were hanging on Candice's every word.

'What you got to say for yourself? I'm waiting,' Candice said.

She'd got Candice's attention so she was off the starting block. What she needed now was a clue. Without more information, Kal didn't know how to craft her pitch and if she got it wrong, this woman would strike like a viper and the others would follow. All she needed was a tiny pointer. So she rubbed her forearms as if she was cold. With an expert gaze, she looked at a couple of the low-ranking women in the circle. Then she let her gaze contact the most susceptible woman in the group, purple-streak. It was a silent plea for help. *Don't let me down, come on, take the bait.*

'If something doesn't happen around here soon, I'll die of boredom,' said one of the women behind Kal.

'Keep your panties on, it'll get busy later.'

Snickers ran around the circle. They were losing interest. Soon they'd fan out to cover the length of the street. She must act soon or she'd be walking away with nothing.

'Are you any good at dancing?' asked purple-streak.

Bingo.

'I love belly-dancing, you know, oriental stuff. I'm pretty good at it – won a couple of awards.'

Kal began circling her hips, sultry and slow. Then she raised her hands and let them Arabic dance across the air. Her mother had practised belly dancing for years and Kal had tried plenty of the moves. She finished with a shoulder shimmy. It was all a lie but with a barrel full of guts you can go a long way – subterfuge and infiltration relied on it.

Candice did a slow clap. 'Not bad, at least, better than a cow in labour. Punters like a bit of something different.'

Candice walked around Kal as if she were assessing an animal at auction. 'Ever taken your clothes off in public?'

It would be easy to lie, only she was pretty certain it wouldn't gain her much.

'No.'

Still, something made Candice hesitate.

'You seem in good shape. And like I said, you've a body for it, mind you why the hell should I stick my neck out for a know-nothing, green runt like you?'

'Because I'm a great dancer and,' Kal cast an admiring glance at Candice's legs and gave a saucy smile, 'because I like your boots?

Candice guffawed. 'Because you can lick my boots more like. I like a girl who can crack a laugh and I like a girl with spirit. It can get as dull as a morgue around here some days. Okay, you do exactly what I say and don't try to get smart. It's your lucky day. I'm taking you to Sugar G.'

Chapter Six

At Lilac Mansions

Night lights lit the path and Sophie followed the line of little lamps.

Her sequin-covered dress rustled. Damp air brought goose bumps to her arms, or was it the adrenalin and the anticipation that made her hot and cold at the same time?

The gardener kept the path weed-free and as clear as the day when it had been laid all those years ago, except, over time, he'd become less forceful pruning the bushes. Many of them now reached over Sophie's height, though she remembered when her mother first planted them as little bundles of earth and a few sprouting stalks.

Ivy brushed her skin and her breath caught as the cold leaves dragged over her shoulder. Then she laughed at herself and carried on. No one else would be here, not yet. *Tack. Tack.* Her steps sounded firm as she approached the front door.

Inside her clutch bag, with one hand she kept a firm grasp on the pepper spray as she searched for the house key. She would be the first to arrive, she knew that. No need to get jumpy.

Standing in the old, family house, it smelled musty and stale. *Click.* She turned on the lights, and turned to face the huge mural painted on the side wall by her mother.

Charlotte Kendrick had painted a mass of blue and purple and lilac flowers, the blossoms tumbling as if they fell from the sky. Her mother told Sophie she'd painted it during her first year in her new home. It had gone hand-in-hand with how they'd named their new house "Lilac Mansions". Charlotte had planned the gardens to be full of lilacs and roses and lavender – a beautiful, English garden full of sweet scents, just as she'd always wanted.

Sophie reached out to stroke the petals of a rose. She took a long in-breath as if she could inhale its scent, or maybe the scent of Charlotte. She swallowed down the sadness. Tonight, she mustn't let it get in the way. Nothing must get in the way.

The house seemed untouched. Behind the door, a black umbrella waited in its stand. The dull shine of the floor spoke of a clean by the housekeeper and Sophie was pleased to see Raymond was keeping his promise to maintain it. The only problem was it felt unlived in. And it smelled of neglect.

Ahead, her father's one extravagance swept up to the top floor – a staircase as if from a Hollywood movie, more fit for an elegant villa than an English house in the countryside. Her father insisted on the staircase because he'd always dreamed of one, and this was supposed to be a house of dreams. It had turned into a house of nightmares.

31

Her dress rustled as she mounted the steps - one, two, three, four. On the fifteenth step, she faltered. This was where it happened. She broke out in a cold sweat as bad memories shifted into focus – she'd been carried down the stairs by a policeman. She remembered his face, older than her father's. Remembered the strange, petrol-like smell of his uniform. And that her cheek was pressed against one of his coat buttons. She remembered too, that it looked like carrying her was making him want to cry. He'd held her tight as he walked across the hallway. She'd wanted to look back, to see into the living room but she'd not been able to move one inch. He must have done that on purpose. So she wouldn't see all the blood. Except that didn't stop Sophie seeing it in her nightmares – on the walls, soaked into the furniture and, worst of all, the streaks where her mother had tried to drag herself away.

Chapter Seven

Candice took Kal to number forty-one. On the outside, it was shabby. On the inside it was a game-players paradise, with the lounge housing wall-to-wall screens and the surfaces jammed with games consoles. There were the remains of a take-away supper and the scents of spicy foods hung in the air.

Candice explained Sugar G was an avid player and she warned Kal not to touch anything. The room was set up for a three-dimensional experience. What types of games interested Sugar G? War, fantasy, or something more sinister, like three-dimensional adult snuff movies or child porn? Kal was making it her business to find out.

As she thought, Sugar G was the women's pimp. He was black, tall and gangly and his arms hung at his sides as if he was missing a few brain cells. This was a front, because Sugar G was sharp as a razor and he assessed Kal in a few blinks of his dark eyes. She knew he didn't buy her story. And she knew he didn't like her.

Neither did Kal like Sugar G. Hiding yourself as a simpleton was a clever trick and not an easy one to pull off because sooner or later most violent men had to strike, had to show their strength just to prove who was in charge. Sugar G kept himself well hidden behind his disguise yet Kal felt the edge in him.

It was an edge of tension, evident at the back of his eyes and in the way he held himself. This man had an edge ready to cut. A dangerous man if you rattled his cage. The type likely to slash first and ask questions later. Kal pegged Sugar G as a knife man. For sure, he'd keep one on him at all times.

Question was, did Sugar G attract a line of men willing to pay big money to rape underage girls? Careful not to grit her teeth, nor even press her lips together, Kal kept her posture soft. She'd got her foot in the door and now she needed to play the part for Sugar G. He must see her as inexperienced. Someone he could reel in at his leisure and manipulate. She gave Sugar G her most innocent smile, one she'd practised for hours in the mirror until it met her father's satisfaction.

'It doesn't look to me like you need it,' Sugar G said.

His left eyelid drooped and a gouge ran just below his eyebrow. Kal presumed he'd almost lost an eye.

'I need cash and I need it quickly.'

'What d'ya need it for?'

'It's personal.'

'No secrets around here,' said Sugar G, 'you can tell your daddy anything.'

'Leave the poor kid alone. She says she's a good mover and I reckon she might be,' Candice said.

'You reckon do you? What I reckon is ever since dip-headed Melanie over-dosed, there's been a hole in the show and my profit's pouring through faster than shit down a toilet. Melanie was pure talent and I told you to keep an eye on her.'

Sugar G stabbed an accusing finger at Candice and the woman flinched.

'Take off your jacket,' Sugar G said.

Kal complied, shrugging it from her shoulders.

He beckoned her over and he leant his face to her neck, stopping just short of Kal's skin. A strap from her top slipped off her shoulder and she controlled the urge to deck him. Sugar G lingered, seemingly inhaling her scent and Kal could hear the sound of her own pulse thumping.

From him, she smelt musk and coffee with no trace of cigarettes, nor alcohol. His t- shirt showed clean forearms with the veins intact - so Sugar G wasn't a drugs man. That made him more clever, since it gave no one a lever they could use over him.

Sugar G held her close as he took in the scent of her hair. Kal worked hard to keep in role. Prostitutes were compliant with their pimp and he'd never take her on if she retaliated. Kal occupied her mind by pondering where he would conceal his knife. With a couple of tiny movements she could have revealed the location of the weapon – for instance by shifting her leg without Sugar G realising, to feel the hilt against her calf, or by draping her arm down his back to where the indent in the material would tell of a hilt stuck in the back of his belt, inches below her fingertips.

Over Sugar G's shoulder, Kal scanned the room. Massive screens, a tangle of leads across all surfaces. A low, glass table was covered in old food containers. It looked like Sugar G was a big Thai food fan. Dark roller blinds hung at every window. As Kal's gaze swept to the corner of the room, a tingle ran up her spine. A man's jacket had been placed over the back of a chair. Under the jacket, a red strip of material peeped out, the end decorated with a fringe. It was Sophie's scarf.

Sugar G finally moved away and, as he did, Kal caught a flash in his eyes, partly of lust and partly of something altogether more violent. It was quickly gone and Kal knew better than to stare.

Sugar G gave her a smile, totally lacking in laughter. He ran his finger down her cheek and Kal wondered if he threatened to scar his girl's faces if they didn't comply.

'You smell sweet and spicy. You sure you want a job?'

'Certain.'

She gave him her practised smile again, though with this man, she wasn't sure he totally bought it.

'Maybe you've got something worth having after all – so you get one chance and only one – you can have the six o'clock slot. It's the warm up before the main event. Show us what you've got and then you and I can get together and have another chat.'

Chapter Eight

I knew I was passing time until I got older. Until the time came for me to do something daring and brilliant.

In my better moments, I knew my thinking was wrong. More than that, I knew I was wrong. But I also realised it was only a matter of time before I crossed the line. The line we all know exists. The line that keeps us sane. The one which means we can call ourselves 'normal' or 'decent'.

My childhood experiments showed me how wonderful it was to inflict pain.

Until I made my move into the real world, I studied police techniques. I read all the police manuals so I know everything about how they search for evidence and DNA. I'm clever. Too clever for them.

I'm a careful planner these days because I have to keep one step ahead of being caught. That first time, I wasn't so careful.

I picked out a young woman – low on confidence, longing for a lover, no real friends to speak of, a bit short of cash. She had a wistful quality about her – someone who had hopes for her future, who believed her dreams would come true and good things would come her way, that all she had to do was wait and along would come her opportunity to step up in the

*world. It was that wistful quality I found so magnetic.
Because what was going to come her way? Me.*

*Tracey worked in a coffee shop by day and as a waitress
in a pizza bar most evenings. Attractiveness wasn't one of my
criteria, though she wasn't unattractive – with a pleasing bra
size and a liking for short skirts even though she had chunky
legs. I became a regular at the coffee shop, telling her I was a
student (true) of mathematics (not true) and that I hated my
family (true) who were stinking rich (also true).*

*Anyway, cut to the chase – I invite her to my apartment.
I suggest we have a bath as part of our pre-sex games. Tracey
readily agrees. When she's in the bath, I give her a neck
massage and then I work my magic as only I can do. It's a
special gift. Quite rare. Then quick as a fox, I get a ligature
around her neck and tighten it enough to make her
uncomfortable. She's still breathing and she's terrified.*

*That first time is still so vivid – the excitement was like a
shot straight in the vein. I practically drooled. With the
ligature in place I give her an injection to keep her tranquil.
Then I cut off her eyelids. By that time, I was deft with the
scalpel. Then I wait for Tracey to come round a little. When
she does, she begs, she pleads. I'm careful to mist her eyes
because I don't want them to dry out and ruin her vision –
she has to see me properly. Up until then, she thought she had
a chance. That I was a sadist but she'd get away with her life.
Wrong. I strangle Tracey and I enjoy her struggle and the
way she stares up at me, unable to blink and not able to block
out the experience even for a second. I am entirely and utterly
the last thing she sees and absorbs before her death.*

*As her life ebbed, Tracey pleaded with her eyes for mercy.
That moment felt pivotal. So much more than animal lust or*

sex or gratification from pain, so much more transcendent. I knew I'd found my true purpose and reason for being on this earth.

Chapter Nine

Kal locked herself in the toilet. She groaned, resting her forehead in her hands. Thanks to years of David Khan's training, she could handle violence and guns and keep her cool around psychopaths and hired killers. But in agreeing to take part in Sugar G's Girly Show she might have met her match.

She needed courage and she needed ideas, so she scanned videos on her phone. The videos made it look easy and Candice told Kal she wasn't supposed to strip. The strippers were in the main part of the show and Kal was the warm up. Still, shit and double shit. She pressed her thumbs onto her eyelids. Would helping Sophie do a little to atone for her father's sins? He'd shed so much blood, surely she was asking for the impossible. But what if it helped, just a bit? What if she really had skills which could help others? What if she could really make a difference?

Kal made her way to the women's changing area.

Though the houses in Montgomery Road seemed separate, four of the properties had been merged together. This created a huge Pleasure Palace with a jacuzzi and sauna area, ground floor night club, stage and bar, and a suite of private rooms.

The first floor was used by the show girls for changing before the nightly cabaret. The top floor was the domain of a woman called Lady Penelope who managed appointments for the girls, whilst Sugar G looked after them on the street.

Around her, a gaggle of women were getting dressed for the show, chatting and gossiping. Kal stood in front of a costume rack, scanning the feathers, the sequins and the scanty costumes. Wafts of perfume and smoke were catching at the back of her throat. Two girls were standing by the window having their last drags on a cigarette and the rest of them were drenched in clouds of different types of scent.

A woman called Tamara came up to Kal's shoulder. She smelled of vanilla. 'For goodness sake, hurry up! You're the first out. All the costumes on this rack are gonna fit, I already told you they're for girls your size.' Tamara took hold under her own bra and bounced her breasts up and down.

'Right,' Kal said.

'I'm gonna help you out before Candice comes back and goes berserk. If there's a problem you can always get sewn into the thing, it only takes a couple of stitches.'

Tamara pulled out what looked like a two-piece lingerie set. She held it up.

'Try this one. Turquoise is a good colour for you and these strings of hanging beads are gonna look great against your legs.' Tamara jiggled the costume so the beads made a sound like water.

'They'll look good when you shimmy.'

'Yeah.'

Tamara laughed. 'First time, right?'

'You got it.'

'Try focusing on the cash.'

'I'm trying, except terror keeps getting in the way.'

Tamara laughed again. 'Get this on, you'll be fine. Then let's get you some body art and shimmer and glimmer. Our resident body artist is back with us tonight.'

Once she'd put on the two-piece, Kal shimmied her shoulders in front of the mirror, then shimmied her hips. The dancing didn't bother her, nor was she worried by the flimsy costume, which was no worse than being in a bikini. What got to her was whether she could pull it off with polish. In the videos, the tease and the dancer's expression said it all. She had the theory but what if she froze up? What if she tripped? What if the audience booed? What if there was somebody out there who knew her, like one of her fellow photographers or an off-duty journalist?

As she did her make-up, Kal thought over how women have used sex and allure as a cover in the spy game for decades. In the French resistance they used it during the second world war. It enabled the Allies to hold out against the Nazis. If a woman could use her gender against the enemy to gather intelligence, then it was important to push herself to get on that stage. In this game, it was vital to cover all the bases. She never wanted to be like the man searching for Sophie and walk away for fear of going one step further. Will-

Nothing could have prepared her. A jolt of horror ran from Kal's heels to the top of her head.

She'd seen bodies before, her father had insisted on it, only it had never been like this. And there had never been this type of stink.

A woman lay on the bed. Her body was mutilated and Kal felt certain the woman was dead. *Check the environment, commanded her father's voice.* She spun in a circle and scanned the room, ready for any attack. Nothing. No one else was there. As fast as she could, Kal checked the adjoining bathroom for any signs of danger or threat. Nothing.

Approaching the bedside, she felt a buzz of light-headedness and covered her mouth and nose with her hand. Kal forced herself to look.

The woman's eyelids had been cut off and she stared white eyed towards the ceiling. A huge band of skin had been removed from the woman's abdomen, exposing her intestines and internal organs, and the woman's blood had streamed from her abdomen, soaking the bedding and forming a dark pool on the carpet. Kal searched for a pulse, knowing there was no hope. The murderer had taken time to arrange the victim's hair in a fan-effect. It had been carefully brushed and lacquered out against the pillow, framing her face.

Should she walk away? Leave it to the police and not look back? Pretend she couldn't do anything to help? No – ever since tracking her mother's abductors, she had a drive for outwitting evil murderers. A taste for it. Because protecting the innocent wasn't always enough.

Check the scene while you have the chance, get all the information you can, said the voice in her head. Kal pushed herself through the shock and went into calculating mode.

The heart-shaped double bed was in the middle of the room, decked in red sheets. Shimmering, voile curtains hung from the ceiling to create a cocoon effect around the bed.

Kal saw how the removal of the woman's eyelids had been done with precision. The cuts were neat and smooth – not done in haste, nor with the woman struggling. Was it her imagination, or did something in the woman's eyes tell her the lids had been removed before she died? Kal shuddered.

She recalled how in the olden days, they believed the image of the killer would be imprinted on the victim's eyes as the last thing they'd see. Kal stared deep at the brown irises before she snapped herself out of it. To lie still for a procedure like that, likely the woman had been drugged, though there were no obvious syringe marks and Kal didn't want to disturb the body to investigate further.

The silk, kimono-style gown had been ripped open and the stink was because she'd voided her bowels, as if she'd anticipated her own death. It wasn't possible to know for sure if the skin over the stomach had been cut off before or after death. The amount of blood suggested before with the heart still beating, though Kal hoped it wasn't the case. She noted the ligature marks around the woman's neck.

The facts pointed to several chilling conclusions. No struggle – meaning the victim knew her killer. She was killed in a busy venue – so the killer planned it in advance and got in and out without being seen. And third, whoever did this was calculating, sadistic and, most likely, highly experienced.

This must be Lady Penelope's space and likely it was Lady Penelope on the bed. The victim hadn't fought for her life and why the hell not? The pillows were in place, the sheets weren't torn off the bed. Had she been with a client? How had someone taken her by surprise? Surely the top cat didn't still see punters? Had she been with a lover?

A detail caught Kal's attention and she leant to examine the woman's shoulder. There was a tiny streak of gold paint. Kal glanced at the silver sheen on her own body – all the girls were covered in glitter and shine. The gold trace could have been left by someone lifting up Penelope to check if she was dead, or shaking her to check it she would wake up. Or it could have been left by the killer.

A terrible thought occurred to Kal and she was about to cross to the dresser when someone ran into the room. It was Sugar G. He stopped, staring at the body and Kal noted his lack of repulsion. She heard a small sound in his throat, of surprise or shock. Then there came a flash of violence in his eyes, the same as she'd seen earlier, only this time he didn't bury it.

She felt his rage coming straight at her.

'What the hell! If you're a fucking cop, I'll kill you,' he snarled.

It was a strange thing to say. Why didn't he see her as the potential killer?

'I'm not a cop, I'm not anything. She's dead.'

'I can see she's fucking dead. Get the hell out of here. Leave her alone.'

Sugar G looked like he wanted to kill. The violence rolled off him in waves and she stood her ground and prepared herself for his attack. On the outside, Kal was careful to keep any direct challenge from her eyes. She kept her shoulders and her muscles soft. Those factors, and probably because she was wearing practically nothing, had their effect. At the last moment, Sugar G turned aside and he went to the bed, leaning over the woman. She noticed how careful he was not to touch anything.

'Is she?'

'Yes, she's dead, I checked,' Kal said. 'It's Lady Penelope isn't it?'

The smell of blood and death was getting stronger. She had to get out of here and her thoughts were already turning to Sophie. Penny was Sophie's friend. Sophie mustn't see her.

'Oh no, the police are gonna be all over this place,' Sugar G said.

Sugar G wasn't displaying any horror. Then again, he wasn't trying to play act it, but his reactions didn't seem in sync for someone who'd run into a room and found a woman brutalised. How had Sugar G arrived so soon? Hadn't he been occupied supervising the girls on the street?

Meanwhile, Sugar G had fallen to his knees.

Kal turned her attention back to the room. She knew how to catalogue a crime scene and he was right, there wasn't much time before the police arrived.

On the other side of the room were two lush, red velvet settees with the backs shaped into a giant pair of lips. There were no windows, so whoever had done this had entered and exited by the main corridor. The décor, the colour choices and the ceiling-drop sheer curtains created an effect much like you'd seen in an old film reproduction of a harem. Kal noted that, in sync with her name choice, Lady Penelope had a sense of humour. There was nothing on the carpet or the walls; no blood stains, no signs of a struggle, no rips or scrapes and no marking from fingernails or metal. Kal went to check the ensuite bathroom. Toiletries and cosmetic products covered every surface. The elegant bath had gold taps and golden feet. The shower cubicle was dry. And there was a pervasive, faint smell of bleach which meant whoever killed Lady Penny had time to wipe down the surfaces.

By the time Kal finished her examination, Sugar G had recovered.

'This is a disaster,' he said, and he scrambled to his feet and ran out the room.

As soon as he'd gone, Kal took a tissue from the dresser and in a couple of careful wipes, she removed the gold smear.

***

She must get to Sophie quickly, before the girl got to hear about it. Leaving the body, she sprinted along an empty corridor and down to the first floor. Evacuation of the property seemed to be the priority. All around, women were rushing to collect their belongings and the dressing room was in pandemonium. Kal grabbed a woman's arm.

'Have you seen Sophie? Has anyone seen Sophie?'

The rainforest room was empty. Systematically, she searched any space large enough to hide Sophie. Nothing. Kal knew she didn't have much time – she'd have to search the whole floor, maybe the entire building. What effect would the murder have on the girl? Not a good one, Kal felt sure. Could Sophie be hiding in one of the rooms on the top floor? Had she made a run for it and was long gone? No, she didn't think so, she felt sure Sophie would seek shelter somewhere she felt safe. But this *was* where Sophie felt safe. Dammit, Kal didn't know the place well enough to pin point where a terrified girl might hide.

Back in the dressing room, they'd all made a run for it and it looked like a swarm had descended, scattering garments so the whole floor was covered in clothes. Stage shoes lay abandoned in the mess, and water bottles and spilt, soft drink cans. The women had taken their personal belongings and dropped everything else. Kal knew she should give up. She'd left traces of her

DNA upstairs when she checked Penelope's pulse and the best thing to do was get out.

Her clothes sat in her locker space. Kal pulled them on and tossed her costume onto the floor. As she bent to tie her shoes, she spotted a large laundry basket sitting in the corner of the room. Rectangular and made of wicker, the stage costumes must usually go in there after the performance.

The hairs on the back of Kal's neck prickled and her fingers stopped mid-lace. She stood up slowly, feeling a stab of panic as her mind turned over the idea. *No, surely not.* Her mouth went dry.

Kal threw up the lid. Sophie was scrunched in the bottom of the basket. The girl lay face down, knees bent up to her chest, arms positioned to protect her head.

Kal closed her eyes. Was she too late? Had whatever the girl was running from caught up with her? No, please, no. She reached in to touch Sophie's shoulder. When she touched skin which was body temperature, the wave of relief was physical.

It took all her coaxing to get Sophie to uncurl and she had to lift the girl out. Sophie was in a total state of shock, unable to speak and with her muscles rigid. Kal knew as soon as Sophie let go she'd start screaming. Sophie had fled to somewhere dark and cramped and made herself as small as possible, so danger didn't come after her, and so she could screw herself up against all the terror. Whatever had sent Sophie into that state, it had been something dreadful.

Kal pulled Sophie towards the door and the girl tottered like a skittle, though she didn't resist. When they got to the corridor, Sophie made a desperate grab for the door frame and wouldn't let go.

'Listen to me. We've got to get out of here and I know you understand why, please don't make me prise your fingers off one by one.'

Actually, her easiest option would be to knock Sophie unconscious. Pressure at the carotid artery would do it. Then she could carry her out much faster. But if she did, Sophie would never trust her again.

Sophie's eyes darted towards the rainforest door and it took a moment for Kal to flick through the possibilities.

'It's the bloody cat, isn't it?'

Even in a deeply traumatised state, a person has the capacity to care for someone more vulnerable than themselves, for instance, a younger sibling. Or a pet.

The ginger cat was curled up in its basket and she grabbed the whole lot. As they headed for the back entrance, they heard the sound of the police sirens.

Chapter Eleven

During the drive back to apartment 701, Sophie hunched in the passenger seat, shaking and clutching the cat's basket.

Post-traumatic stress disorder – she'd already seen it in Sophie at the roadside. This was a second bout. Had the news been enough to trigger it? Or did it mean she'd seen Penny dead?

She kept alert to Sophie's status, in case the trauma shifted and Sophie launched into a break-down. It would only take a tiny thaw, and all the emotion would come like a tidal wave. Kal kept her cool. She thought over the crime scene, checking her conclusions. The most important question was motive. Find the motive and you find the killer. Why had Penny been killed? And why now? And what was Sophie's part in this?

They reached the apartment.

'Hold on, Sophie. We're almost there'.

The girl made no sign she'd heard and Kal removed the seat belt. She anticipated getting Sophie in the lift might cause a problem, where perhaps the feeling of being trapped would be enough to cause the melt-down. It didn't, and the two of them arrived at the top of the building. Then, as the blanket slipped from

Sophie's shoulders and Kal closed the front door, it started.

Sophie fell to the floor. She kicked her legs and struck out blindly. Kal put her arms as loose and as strong as she could around Sophie to stop her hurting herself as she banged against the floor and off the walls. Sophie screeched at the top of her voice and Kal hung on. Sophie's stamina would not last for long. When the animal noises subsided, Sophie switched to screaming.

'He's coming!' She screamed. 'He's coming to get me!'

Using her own body as a cushion, could only wait for Sophie to come back to the here and now. When the wild terror finally faded, she went limp and began sobbing.

'You're safe now. I've got you. You're safe.'

Sophie clung to Kal's clothing. 'No, please don't let him.'

Poor Sophie. Whatever trauma Sophie had lived through in the past, it had been retriggered big-time at the Pleasure Palace. Sophie had re-experienced the same terror and the same helplessness she'd known in the past. Just like with combat veterans and survivors of abuse, retriggering was one aspect of Post-Traumatic Stress Disorder.

'You're safe here, I promise you're safe. Look at me, Sophie. You're with me and you're safe.'

The girl was shaking so hard, her teeth chattered. 'Oh god, oh please, help me.'

'I promise I will,' Kal said. And she meant it.

She half-carried Sophie into the lounge and put her on the settee. Very sensibly, the cat had bolted to some dark corner and wasn't available as a comforter. Kal tucked Sophie up with a blanket and sat cuddling her.

When she sensed she could, she made hot chocolate. Sophie held on to the mug as if it was a lifeline, though she made no effort to drink it. As the last of the emotion drained away, Kal knew she must break the bad news about Penny. It wouldn't be fair to put it off until later. No, she must tell Sophie now. Kal steeled herself. This would feel like cruelty, like twisting the knife.

Sophie's head lolled. 'Did you get to see your friend?' she whispered.

'You're exhausted, Sophie, and, yes, I got to see Marty…'

Sophie seemed to sense Kal's hesitation. 'Was she okay?'

'Listen, there's something terrible I need to tell you and it's about Penny.'

'Penny?'

When Kal took hold of Sophie's hands, the girl snatched them away.

'Penny!'

'There's no good way to say this and I'm so sorry. Lady Penny is dead. She's been murdered.'

If there'd have been anything left to spill, it would have come out. Except there were no tears left, no strength to sob, not enough force to speak. The shock was total. Sophie moved her mouth and nothing came out and Kal could hear Sophie's dry lips touching and opening.

'I'm so sorry. I know she was your friend.'

Kal also knew what she had to say and do next and that it would come as a sucker punch to poor Sophie. But Kal had no choice, not if she was going to pin down the killer. So she forced it out.

'And I've got to get back there and find out more.'

This was exactly the right moment to go back to Montgomery Road to pick up information – the place was in chaos and the women too rocked to keep their shields intact. Vital intelligence would be available right now that would disappear within the space of a few hours. Correct questioning and scouting around had to happen quickly.

'I know it's a terrible shock and I wish I could stay with you. There are things I can do back there – I'm good at that kind of thing, experienced. I can't explain it right now but you'll have to take my word on it. I need to go back to Montgomery.'

Kal plumped the cushions. She tried not to feel guilty and failed, though she knew if she didn't get back there soon, after the police interrogations and the general traffic of forensics, detectives and the rest of the crime squad, there'd be nothing left except denials and dust.

Comforting Sophie would have to go on hold. And Sophie's memory would have to wait. This wasn't the right time to delve into the events of the evening or of the past. Once they started trying to unpack that hornet's nest, they'd open up something that could take days or weeks to resolve.

Sophie bit her lip.

'We're on the seventh floor, Sophie. It's the top and it's got a steel safety door and no one can get to you, you understand?'

There was fear in Sophie's eyes. Shit, this was horrible. She put her hand on Sophie's arm.

'I'm going to come back and be with you but first I need to get back to Montgomery. It's important. I can help nail Penny's killer.'

Sophie looked away.

'I know this is hard and I'm sorry. I wouldn't leave you if it wasn't absolutely necessary.'

The nod of Sophie's head was almost imperceptible. Kal hadn't expected it. Oh gosh, this girl had real guts.

Before she could change her mind, Kal tucked the blanket more firmly around Sophie, turned on the lamp beside the settee and stepped away. She had to take the chance. Sophie was fragile but she felt sure the girl had inner reserves. People who lived through hardship always did have. If Sophie dug deep, she could feel safe enough, perhaps not safe enough to fall asleep but then the exhaustion would play its part. No harm would come to her.

Touring the flat, she made sure all the blinds were down, hunting in vain for the cat. It had disappeared, so Sophie would have to cope on her own. At the steel door, Kal hesitated one final time and leant her forehead against the cool surface. Yes, this felt horrible, but she was making the right decision. Kal wrenched open the door and ran down the stairs before she could change her mind.

Chapter Twelve

In the cold night air, Kal felt a skip of excitement. The front line was her element. A place she could test herself and use her expertise to the full.

Patrol cars were pulled up at the end of Montgomery and their flashing lights illuminated a deserted street. Instead of scurrying to see what all the fuss was about, the locals had locked themselves inside, signalling them to be the type of Londoners who prefer to remain anonymous, who came to the big city to be sucked up. This wasn't the suburbs, where curious, middle class on-lookers would have to be held back by the police. No, this was the dark underbelly of the city, where life was cheap.

An ambulance was parked behind one of the police cars and its back doors swung free. No medic personnel were in sight, which meant they must be upstairs with the body, maybe waiting for forensics to arrive.

The pavement sounded damp under Kal's shoes. With long strides, she made her way in the direction of two police officers – one of them was posted at the entrance to number thirty-three and the other at number thirty-five. Both officers were alert and running on a high, she could see it in their faces. A murder

He was pushing his weight onto her. Neighbour's lights lit the far end of the garden and didn't reach as far as the two of them. All Kal could see was Sugar G's outline as he leaned on her chest. She concentrated on the tone of his voice. It changed when he talked about Sophie and she needed to know why.

'Sophie? What is it about her?'

This was risky. She wasn't behaving the right way. Sugar G was used to obedient women. Women who needed him for protection on the streets. Even this slight resistance from her put him further on edge. Kal could sense it. Sense how he couldn't stand her asking even this simple question. Danger sparked off him like electricity.

Kal saw Sugar G's hand go behind his back. In preparation to strike back, she took a slow breath in. He reached towards his belt and she felt the calm which trickled into him as soon as he had his hand on the hilt of his weapon. Now he felt in control. Kal readied herself. She wasn't afraid, though she knew he'd be fast and deadly, and he'd think later, once it was all over. Kung fu couldn't save her from everything, but it gave her a huge advantage, and one which most opponents had no idea was coming their way. Even with her injured knee, it should give her enough time to get away.

As the seconds ticked and Sugar G changed his grip on the knife, she decided to take one more risk.

'And what about Sophie's brother? He was looking for her too.'

'That bastard. If he doesn't stay away from her I swear I'll-'

At that moment, a light flashed on inside the closet. A shout came from inside and someone, most likely a police officer, poked their head out of the window.

Sugar G didn't wait. He dropped Kal like a sack of potatoes and sprinted off. Kal ran in the opposite direction. When she got to the fence, she crawled on her belly to the corner. Her heart hammered.

'Wait out your enemy', commanded the voice in her head.

Kal didn't stir until her breathing went back to normal. There was no sign of Sugar G and she didn't want to run into him again, not yet anyway. His last answer was interesting – Sugar G hated Sophie's brother. But why? And why was Sugar G so invested in Sophie in the first place?

She needed to speak to Sophie. The mystery around the girl was deepening and the further Kal dug the more dangerous it felt.

All was quiet. She vaulted into the neighbouring garden, then vaulted a couple more fences and slid into the road running parallel to Montgomery. She crouched, listening. A radio sounded from an open window and a dog barked several streets away. A car drove past, and when the road was silent again, Kal made her way to the end of the street and back to 701.

Chapter Fourteen

At Lilac Mansions

Keeping the pepper spray tight in one hand, Sophie opened the door to her childhood bedroom.

The room smelled of herbs. Or was that her imagination? Everything seemed untouched – frozen in time – a snapshot of her life as a child. Of the moment before everything fell apart.

Sophie ran her hand along the titles on the bookshelf. Since her breakdown, she'd only been back here a few times. Each visit reminded her of her previous life.

Her fingers rested on the covers; the bright colours of a famous author, then a row of much-loved titles with tattered dustcovers, then slimmer books, then fatter ones. Sophie lingered on her childhood favourites. She loved reading. After the night both her parents died, losing herself in stories became her escape. These shelves contained the books she couldn't bear to part with, except they hadn't been enough to sustain her, and they'd certainly not been enough to keep away the pain.

After her parents were killed, there had been a mourning period and then they expected Sophie to go back to school. Often, she pretended to have tummy aches and took to bed for days on end. It had been easy with the string of au pairs and with everyone in a mess and walking around Sophie like she was made of egg-shells.

No one spoke to her about the deaths, or the bodies, or the funerals, or the emptiness and dread she felt inside. They didn't talk to her about the police investigation, or the questions and the suspicions.

Raymond, her legal guardian at age twenty-one, had been ill-equipped to bring up a young child on his own. Sophie remembered how he spent most of his time elsewhere. When he was home, Raymond avoided her in the big house. They never ate together and on the rare occasions they crossed paths he didn't meet her eye. Sophie spent her time trailing behind the au pairs and that's how life continued.

There'd been plenty of trips to the doctor to fathom the reasons for her feigned sicknesses. Then Raymond sent her to boarding school until, age eleven, she'd had a panic attack in the assembly hall. It came right in the middle of a presentation for the parents. Sophie was supposed to be reciting a poem. She remembered Raymond's eyes watching her as she walked to the lectern and the next thing she knew, she was on her knees and fighting to breathe. After a few moments of general alarm, the ambulance came to take her away.

With the stands packed with adults it had been her ultimate humiliation. Though in truth, it was the end result of many episodes locking herself in the toilets and bouts of sobbing to which no one paid much attention.

When she thought about it now, Sophie wondered how she'd held out so long.

She'd already been going to see Dr Kaufman for outpatient sessions and after the meltdown she became a permanent resident at Melrose clinic. Dr Kaufman was a good friend of her father, and Raymond had grasped his offer of help with both hands.

Sophie pulled "The Diary of Anne Frank" from the shelf and stared at the black and white photograph of Frank. It was the last book she read before her breakdown. Since then, she'd been schooled by a private tutor.

Lilac Mansions lay silent, waiting, Sophie thought, for the final instalment – for the closing of the circle and her coming of age all in one blow.

Bending to smooth the covers of the bed, Sophie fancied she caught a faint scent of rosemary. She'd so loved to pick handfuls from the garden and keep jars of drying herbs in her room – mint, thyme and rosemary. That terrible night, the scent of rosemary had been strong because Charlotte had tucked a sprig of it under Sophie's pillow.

Taking a deep breath, she breathed in the smell of rosemary. Yes, she'd been woken by voices downstairs. There had been shouting. She recognised her father's voice and how he sounded angry in a way she'd never known before. The violence frightened her and though part of her wanted to keep away, she'd been drawn to the sounds of her mother in the background, talking calmly as if to soothe her father.

Why she'd got out of bed, she couldn't say. Curiosity probably. The need to know more. The need to find out about the adult world and discover what secrets they kept tucked away. Being light on her feet, she thought she could sneak closer without being seen and then run back to bed. That had been her first mistake.

Chapter Fifteen

Growing up hiding my secret wasn't as difficult as you might imagine.

My parents, rich and self-obsessed, spent their vacations in exotic places – Greece, Italy, Canada, the Bahamas. And I was left behind with an au pair.

I was of no interest to them except to show off my academic talents and progression up the achievement ladder. I grew up cold and alone in a house full of riches. Now isn't that an irony?

I didn't muse on the origins of love until I became a student. The normal emotions of the world meant nothing to me and so I considered love to be amongst those items to be discarded for me in this lifetime. In fact, I felt nothing but pity for my peers who lolled on their beds or moped around the dormitories struck down by wonder for some rather ordinary person, usually, but not restrictively, of the opposite gender.

Charlie changed all that.

She had a grace which stopped me in my tracks. And she had that wonderful, magnetic wistfulness in abundance – a woman who believed all her dreams would come true.

I knew I wanted it all fixated on me.

I imagined her blonde hair tumbling onto the bed and her eyes staring into mine, filled with awe and desperation and terror.

Charlie would be my second victim and I realised she'd be more of a challenge than my previous target. She had confidence and no lack of admirers and so I set about planning how I would make her mine.

This didn't make any sense. But Sophie's panic was real. Kal propelled her to the bathroom.

'Lock yourself in,' she said. 'You'll be able to hear everything and I'll tell you when it's okay to come out. There's absolutely nothing to worry about.'

Against all logic, the pit of Kal's stomach had turned cold and, though she couldn't fathom why, she wished she had her gun. It was stashed in its usual hiding place at the training centre. Perhaps she should go back soon and get it.

Kal crossed quickly to the window. A white florist's van was pulled up outside. Kal had learned to trust her instincts and they were on red alert, even though the van appeared completely normal. Her pulse notched up.

As she waited for the knock at her door, she flexed her knees and felt a pain shoot up her left leg. The hit-and-run while searching for her mother had a lot to answer for. At the end of her physiotherapy treatment, the therapist had told Kal to give it time and go easy on the martial arts, that knees could take a long time to heal after an injury, even when all the x-rays and imaging showed them to be in shape. In response, Kal had told the therapist something rude, which she later regretted.

The knock was short and sharp. Kal checked the spy-hole. A young man was on the other side, holding a bouquet of what looked like white lilies.

'Hello,' he said brightly, 'please sign here.'

He pushed a digital pad into Kal's hands. He was in a rush, his mind already on his next call. Once she'd signed, he passed over the flowers and was already starting for the elevator when he called over his shoulder. 'There's a card inside.'

She'd got ruffled up for nothing. Why did she let Sophie's panic get to her? It wasn't like her. The man was a florist and he'd not come with any sinister intentions.

She closed the door and took out the small card. When she read it, she fell to her knees, crushing the lilies to her chest.

"We knew you'd be consumed by the need for revenge.

We decided to save you the trouble."

The Cartel had sent flowers. Kal hunched over the lilies and stared at the numbers beneath the message.

It was a London map reference.

Chapter Seventeen

A grey sky hung over the river Thames. It looked like another summer storm was on its way. Across the water, office blocks faced onto the shoreline, and it was so odd to see them with their lights on, warding off the eerie, summer gloom. Kal stared at the little rows of lit squares, trying to fend off her own dark mood. The Cartel had decided to take things into their own hands and it didn't bode well.

She knew it had been a mistake to ever ask for their help. She'd been driven to the point of desperation in the search for her mother, and there had seemed no alternative. She felt sure the florist's card signalled the end of the man who called himself Klaus. The one who tortured her mother.

The map reference led the search party to the Thames just south of Battersea bridge. On this side, it was an empty stretch.

A light but surprisingly bitter wind whipped along the river, chopping up the water and forming white caps. Kal didn't envy the scuba divers their task. They'd suited up without a hint of protest and the four-person team had already been searching for a good hour. It must be freezing down there and she was sure visibility would be close to nil. Detective Inspector Spinks stood by Kal's side. He'd responded to her call straight away.

Detective Inspector Spinks didn't say much and Kal stood like stone, staring out over the water. After all the events earlier in the year, and despite her initial dislike and suspicion of him, Spinks had become someone she admired. At their first meeting, the odds against that had been phenomenal.

What would he think of her if he knew the connection between her and the Cartel? What if he knew the Cartel were responsible for this death? Kal felt angry they presumed to know her feelings, though she knew there was no logic and certainly no compassion in their action. The Cartel was only ever about strategy. And about playing to their own advantage.

Sophie insisted on coming with Kal, despite her own fear of going outside. It was as if she'd adopted Kal as her protector and now the girl waited a short distance away, cold and watchful, squelching about on the bank. The Thames was a tidal river and they stood on the exposed sludge, amongst assorted debris. The mud gave off an unpleasant odour of slime and decay.

DI Spinks cleared his throat. 'You seemed so sure on the phone but you didn't tell me how you got the tip off.'

Kal glanced at Spinks. His jawline was his strongest feature and stamped him out as a man of character. Clean shaven, with greying hair and dark, hooded eyes, Spinks appeared the same – worn down but resilient, saving his energy and endurance. She wondered what

Chapter Eighteen

Marty lay recovering. It had been an exhausting physiotherapy session. She gazed out the window to where a line of trees marked a children's area and a small boy played on the swings and she was about to drift off to sleep when Kal barged in. No knocking? And with a swing in her step? Something had changed for the better. Marty chuckled to herself.

'What're you looking so pleased about?' Kal said.

She tossed a bag of food in Marty's direction.

'I got some of your favourites – I expect they're a bit tight on the treats in this place, aren't they?'

Marty rolled her eyes. 'You're right on that one,' she said and she flung a few cashews into her mouth.

'There's something we need to talk about,' Kal said. 'You know you wondered why I was soaking wet yesterday? I picked up a young girl in trouble and she's staying with me for a while.'

Marty almost choked. 'Oh yeah, of course. You must've undergone a complete character transformation whilst I've been out of it. Inhospitability being one of your strong points.'

'You seem much better, you've got your cutting tongue back.'

'I'll take that as a compliment. Actually, I've been up and about on the treadmill. Apparently, it's like when they send people into space – as soon as you stop using your muscles they lose strength and actual mass, so I'll have to work to get it back. But you know me, workout is my middle name.'

Marty left out the bit about it hurting like hell. She'd been someone who went to sessions of kung fu and ran four times a week. Without use, her muscles hadn't only wasted, her tendons, ligaments and muscles had shortened. Stretching them felt like torture. Regaining her strength and stamina would be hard enough, but Marty felt sure getting back her old flexibility would be by far the hardest part of her recovery. Still, no need to drag Kal down with all of that.

'So what's cooking with this girl?'

'I almost ran Sophie over and then the woman who was sheltering Sophie gets murdered. Penny was killed and her eyelids cut off and her skin cut away to expose her organs and not in that order. I was there and I got to the body and snatched a few minutes to take in evidence. Sophie was downstairs in a catatonic state and we got out together. I'm sure she knows something. She's hiding at my place. I think someone's trying to get to Sophie. Don't know who and I don't know why.'

'Woah!'

Marty stopped delving into the treat bag. Kal attracted trouble like a magnet. It had been the same for as long as they'd known each other – which was a long time – fights at school, fights outside school, rubbing people up the wrong way. And now murder seemed to

96

be becoming her friend's speciality, and Marty didn't like the sound of that, she didn't like the sound of it at all.

'How the hell did you get yourself involved? Can't leave you alone for one second, can I?'

Kal shrugged. 'It just happened.'

'Yeah sure,' Marty said. 'Danger just keeps running towards you, doesn't it? How're you going to cope without me around to watch your back?'

'You are around to watch my back.'

'Not yet I'm not. You haven't seen me try the stairs, and that was going down, goodness knows what I'll be like trying to get up 'em and I'm not exaggerating.'

A small silence fell. Marty didn't want to deflate Kal and neither did she think it right to give her unrealistic hopes. They'd always been close – Kal getting into trouble and Marty bailing her out, smoothing things over, calming people down, but they couldn't be the team they'd been tracking down Kal's mother and facing life and death risks. Not yet anyway.

'Don't look so glum,' Marty said. 'It doesn't mean I'm out of the picture and, amazingly, the docs seem to think I've got all my brain power. So even if I can't be involved in the action, I can work on it behind the scenes. What've you got so far?'

Kal tossed over her phone. 'Sophie's parents were both killed.'

Marty forced herself not to grimace as she pushed herself higher up the bed. She read aloud from the screen.

'"Sophie Kendrick, now aged seventeen. The daughter of Charlotte and Martin Kendrick. Sophie's half-brother, Raymond, is the son of Martin Kendrick by a former wife. Martin Kendrick was a surgeon and a respected consultant at a leading London medical school. He was ten years older than his second wife, Charlotte." Ten years older than Charlotte, that's a big age difference,' Marty said. 'Wouldn't that make Charlotte closer to Raymond's age?'

Kal shrugged.

'"Charlotte died from multiple stab wounds from a frenzied attack. Martin died from a single bullet. The knife which killed Charlotte and the gun were found at the scene, both free from prints. That husband and wife killed each other after a dispute was proposed as a theory. This wasn't supported by the evidence though the police didn't rule it out. Neither did they rule out the presence of a third party, never identified. An open verdict was returned on the killings.

The couple owned a sizeable house in the Surrey countryside, name Lilac Mansions, and they had substantial investments. Raymond and Sophie inherited the estate, it being divided equally between them, with trustees appointed for the administration of Sophie's portion. Sophie's share will be given to her when she reaches eighteen." Right,' Marty said, 'and that's all too long ago. We've got to work with the fresh events.'

'Agreed. The only other useful background is Raymond set up a website to help him in his search for Sophie. This isn't the first time she's run off. His site describes Sophie as vulnerable and it also said she'd

with hatred and savagery. The lines of her face were hardened.

Shit, the girl had changed from light to dark. She was transformed.

Both of them were breathing hard. Kal snapped her fingers in front of Sophie to make sure she wasn't caught in some kind of nightmare. But no, Sophie kept tension in her arm and resisted Kal. And she stared as if Kal was the enemy.

'What the hell's going on,' Kal shouted.

Sophie was no physical match for her and the girl panted with the struggle.

'No point in trying, Sophie, I'm far stronger than you.'

One moment they were locked against each other, and the next Sophie's crazed state of mind slipped away. Her arm collapsed, to leave the Sophie Kal knew – a frail Sophie, full of confusion, full of bewilderment.

Sophie's lips trembled. She started crying and crumpled on the bed.

'Oh no, oh no, I'm s-s-so sorry.'

With her chest heaving and huge sobs, it was clear Sophie's horror was genuine.

What the hell was going on? Kal had to do a reassessment of her own. Did Sophie suffer from some sort of personality disorder? A split psyche? Was there more here than post-traumatic stress disorder? Shit.

Kal pulled Sophie towards her. Now the girl was fragile and frightened. As Sophie sobbed onto Kal's shoulder, Kal felt the girl's torment. How horrible it must be to feel you didn't know who you were. Or what the hell was going on inside you. As she stroked Sophie's hair, a small doubt began to grow. What had she let into her life this time? A cuckoo in the nest? Or something much worse?

'What the hell's wrong with me! I h-hate myself. I hate myself.' Sophie's voice was full of pain.

Chapter Nineteen

Kal had the habit of being a bad sleeper, mostly due to flashbacks to her father's training. So for Sophie to have left the apartment without Kal knowing, meant Sophie was very good at sneaking around.

After the attack, they'd fallen asleep together on Kal's bed. It had been a troubled sleep for Sophie. At first when she awoke, Kal thought Sophie must have snuck away to hide in her corner.

When she didn't find Sophie behind the settee, Kal searched the flat. That's when she found the note on the table. "Please forgive me and please, please look after Purdy."

The cat followed Kal in her search of the apartment and now it regarded her with its green eyes.

'Don't look at me like that. It's not my fault.'

But it was the worst thing that could have happened – Sophie vulnerable and alone. Damn, where would she go? She couldn't hide at Penny's, so did it mean the girl was on the streets? Kal went cold at the thought. Sophie wasn't capable of surviving. Out there, she'd be prey to all kinds of bastards on the prowl for the weak – rapists, murderers, abductors. Vulnerable girls went missing all the time. She must find Sophie, and quickly.

If Marty were better, the two of them could've worked a pattern, covering the area around the apartment and relying on teamwork and efficiency to do the job thoroughly. These first minutes could make all the difference. It was early in the morning and Sophie couldn't have been gone long. If a close proximity search came up empty, they'd face a much wider and more complex set of possibilities.

Kal dressed quickly and made a snap decision. She'd promised herself she'd stay away from LeeMing and, since her knee wasn't up to intensive kung fu, it had been easy to miss out on training. Men who were already taken weren't her style and it was better for her to stay well clear of him. Worse than that, being around LeeMing kept fanning the little flame of hope she felt inside, the one she wanted to deny even existed which said he liked her too.

LeeMing answered the call promptly.

'Hello, I was starting to think you were avoiding me,' LeeMing said.

Kal kept her tone curt. 'As if. I've simply had better things to do and I thought I'd run into you at the hospital.'

'I guess our visiting times haven't coincided.'

No, because LeeMing's visits had been at regular times and she'd avoided them. With Marty in a coma, the last thing she wanted was a moment of weakness with LeeMing and her being dumb enough to confide all the shit she'd discovered about her father. No, that was for Marty's ears only.

She'd decided her tactic mustn't be full frontal – smashing Kendrick up against a wall would give her satisfaction but it wasn't likely to yield the information she needed. No, she must be more clever. Hence the short dress. She would leak intelligence out of him by putting him off his guard. By letting him think he kept his position of moral superiority and by playing on his dislike of Penny and the street workers and their trade.

Kal glanced into the open plan area and spotted only one woman on the team and she was a lot older than the others. That was interesting. Didn't Kendrick like women, or was he a raving sexist when it came to employment?

Since Kal had given Sophie as the reason for her visit, she didn't think Kendrick would keep her waiting long.

She was right. Within a few minutes, Kendrick came personally to the waiting room. Kal took in his appearance in one practised glance. As she'd seen before, features unlike Sophie's and a dress sense with flair, with a tailored shirt and smooth-line jacket. Most notable was the quality of his clothing because it wasn't simply expensive, it was hyper-expensive.

Despite his professional veneer, as he approached Kal, Kendrick had an awkward air about him – the type to have been shy around girls at school, she thought. Or maybe he went to an all-boys school. A man who might attract women yet not be overly aware of it and not know how to deal with it when it came his way. Not all men are passionate. At least, not with women. In Kal's assessment, Kendrick's passion, and therefore his weakness, revolved around wealth and having the finer things of life around him and on his person. Probably he detested the feel of cheap materials on his skin. The sort of man to spend thousands even on his underwear and socks.

He extended his hand. 'Raymond Kendrick,' he said, 'I'm sorry to keep you waiting, thank you so much for contacting me. Let's go through to my office, shall we?'

Though Kendrick concealed it well, she could feel his nervousness. Perhaps he'd been teased for his lack of ability with the opposite sex.

'I'm Karla, but my friends call me Kal,' she said, offering nothing more and noting his questioning look. It didn't seem he remembered her from Montgomery Road, but still he must wonder if she could be a prostitute. Kal had chosen her image to suggest it with a dark red velvet dress which was so short she was glad there was no breeze today. She wore a good layer of makeup too.

His mind would put together Kal's image and Sophie's presence at Montgomery and wonder if Kal could be in the sex trade. As she prepared to stand, she wriggled to the edge of the seat and allowed the hem of her dress to ride up, noting how Kendrick turned away.

Kendrick had a beautiful office with lazure effect walls and concealed downlighting. Even the carpet oozed opulence – Kendrick most likely adored spending ten times as much on his purchases as everyone else. For people with a certain type of personality, it could become an addiction.

Kendrick steered them away from two armchairs arranged next to the window. He indicated a chair in front of his desk. Yes, she thought, he wants the safety of a barrier between us.

'I hope you don't mind if we get straight down to what brought you here. You told me on the phone you have information about Sophie?'

'I'm here for the money, Mr Kendrick. On your website it says there's a reward for information.'

Kendrick pressed his lips together and Kal could almost feel the tension squeezing along his jaw. It told her Kendrick wasn't a generous man.

'Tell me what you know first and then we'll see if it's worth a payment. I think it's the only fair way to proceed, don't you?' he said.

The more Kal got a handle on Kendrick the more she disliked him. She flicked back her hair and the man almost winced. No, he certainly didn't feel comfortable around women.

'I was visiting a friend of mine in Montgomery Road and I saw Sophie there. She's your sister, right?'

'Sophie is my half-sister,' Kendrick said. 'Where exactly did you see her? Did you speak to her? Was she with anyone?'

Kal assessed Kendrick's intonation, the nuances in his facial muscles, the changes in his breathing. This man was eager. If any concern was there, it came as a weaker undercurrent. It didn't seem to her Sophie was his dearly beloved, lost sister. No, any feeling he felt for Sophie was too pinched by his own agenda.

'I overheard Sophie asking for a man called Sugar G and then one of the women took her into a house on Montgomery Road, number forty-one I think. I didn't see her after and I'm sorry I didn't speak to her. Your sister seemed anxious, maybe even afraid. If you like, I can ask my friend to find out more because she knows Sugar G.'

'You're sure it was Sophie?'

'She looked the same as on the flyer and she called herself it, so yeah.'

'And what were you doing in Montgomery Road?'

'Like I said, I went to see my friend and I'm not a prostitute if that's what you're asking.'

Kendrick raised his eyebrows. 'Then what are you?'

Good. He was taking the high ground, looking down on her just as she'd anticipated. It would make him less vigilant.

'I'm an escort and it's completely different. I only work with top-end clients and, for your information, they pay a lot for the privilege of my company.'

Kal injected a spark into her delivery to suggest she might be irritated, but not so much it would put him off, nor make him feel overpowered. She smiled to soften the moment.

'If you're ever in need of a woman to go to dinner with…'

Kendrick's neck flushed red. 'That won't be necessary and I won't be paying anything for your little visit here.'

In Kal's mind she saw Kendrick's wallet snap closed and he even sat up straighter in his seat. It made her think about Sophie's share of the inheritance.

'What you've told me is of no value at all,' he said.

'That isn't fair. I've come all the way to see you. I saw your sister, aren't you worried about her? Aren't you looking for her? You said you were.'

'What you've told me is useless.'

Kendrick was lying. She could tell by his delivery of those few words. Sighting Sophie in Montgomery Road had been of interest to him and so had the mention of Sugar G's name.

Kendrick was on his feet, looking down his nose at her.

'I don't need your information because I know exactly where my sister is. She's back where she should have been all along.'

Kal worked hard to keep herself in role. Shit, why on earth would she have gone back there? It didn't make any sense.

Kendrick pushed back his chair. 'Sophie is safely in the care of Melrose Clinic so please don't bother me with your petty pleading for cash. You won't be getting anything from me.'

His voice was full of greed and satisfaction and Kal's dislike of Kendrick solidified. This man was passive aggressive, full of tightness and frustration and only able to express it in an underhand, nasty way. Sophie would soon be eighteen and then she'd be eligible for her full half of the inheritance. Was Kendrick low enough to threaten his sister in order to gain control of her money? Yes, she thought it very likely.

Let's see what else she could squeeze out before he got rid of her.

'And what about my other offer? Wouldn't you appreciate my glamorous company at one of your high-flying clubs? Or maybe an evening event?' Kal leant forward and gave a sultry smile.

'Certainly n-not. Surely you don't believe I'd have the s-s-slightest interest in a woman like you.'

A flash of spite flared in his eyes and he didn't bother to tone down his disgust and there had come the giveaway, because Kendrick must have been a stutterer. He'd probably spent years in speech therapy to overcome it. The remnant of it reappeared only briefly and specifically in response to her flirtation. Before he overcame the problem, in the company of girls, Kendrick's life must have been a misery.

Kal tossed her hair and stalked out, purposely swaying her backside as she went. She could almost feel Kendrick's paralysis as he stared at her in horror.

Kal wanted to rush straight to Sophie but there was one thing she had to get straight in her mind first. One thing which didn't sit right.

Once outside the building, she found a quiet spot around the side. Leaning against the wall, she closed her eyes and thought about Kendrick, about how he spoke and how he held himself, his choice of words and the feelings she had sitting opposite him. Ideas always came to her this way. It was a tried and trusted method of profiling your target and a technique taught to her in detail. Kal ran through the meeting in her mind, noticing the details, being systematic and putting together the puzzle as if she could see into Kendrick's psyche and pin him out like an insect.

In the background, a car reversed into a parking space. Kal heard it shuffling backwards and forwards, then the *thunk* of car doors. Two people chatted as they walked past, one woman and one man. Then the street grew quiet. A few moments later, Kal's eyes snapped open.

A nasty, cold feeling had settled at the back of her neck. She felt certain her insight about Kendrick was spot on – Kendrick didn't just feel anxious around women, he hated them.

Chapter Twenty-one

Given the differences between us you might have thought it would be difficult for me to attract Charlie's attention. Not so. She was someone who enjoyed a bit of clandestine activity, as I was soon to find out. We began dating in secret. As I told you, I can play the part. She seemed impressed by my academic achievements and by my insipid jokes.

I began manoeuvring Charlie into position to be my second victim.

Any novice can slip up, and this is when I made a serious error. Like with Tracey, I should've worked on Charlie quickly. I didn't, and it meant she started messing with my mind. How could someone as disciplined and single-minded as me be thrown off course by their own target? I can't explain, except to say I allowed Charlie to live for month after month, and the longer she survived, the more I allowed myself to weaken and prolong her life.

This wasn't a delay of anticipation and meticulous planning, though I think I told myself it was. As I watched her and followed her and mapped out her life, I wondered about obsession, because to me she was like an angel. An angel who walked the earth.

One evening, I even went into a church and stared up at saints in the stained-glass windows. They were beautiful, like Charlie, with glowing halos.

I stayed all night though I didn't pray, and something about me prevented anyone from approaching, even the pastor. It can't be true that I thought about being saved. I don't have a conscience, you see. I don't care. I am without empathy. Every feeling is a pretence. An act. But something kept me rooted on that hard bench like a penitent. If anyone could save me, Charlie could, and part of me knew that.

What would I choose, salvation or damnation? The battle raged in me month after month, and made me falter like a weakling. Because inside, don't we all want to be rescued from the horrible parts of life? From the horrible parts of ourselves? Yes, even the monsters of this world like me.

And that delay in taking Charlie's life would cost me.

Chapter Twenty-two

Being born in London, Kal knew the city could be infuriating, chaotic and wonderful all at the same time. The sun was doing its best to show through scattered clouds. A mass of people dashed here and there like crazed things, amidst zillions of cars and buses. Kal joined the rush.

Melrose Clinic was in the rich district of Westminster, on a stretch near Harley Street. Harley Street had a worldwide reputation for private care, being prized by the rich and famous for a range of health services and cosmetic surgery.

Getting from The Strand to Harley Street gave her time to research Melrose Clinic. She tried to puzzle out why Sophie would return to the place she'd said she hated. The best guess Kal came up with was Sophie spent so many years at the clinic, she'd become institutionalised.

Institutionalised patients couldn't cope with normal life. With life outside. They'd spent so long incarcerated, they became unable to function for long outside the rules and safety and routine of the place looking after them. In the olden days, institutionalisation in long-term hospitals meant patients became stripped of the skills, and even the desire, to live in society.

The idea sat uncomfortably. She'd seen Sophie as a young woman struggling for her freedom. Being confined didn't fit with the picture and hadn't Sophie specifically said she felt watched all the time at Melrose? Trapped?

With a team of over twenty consultant psychiatrists, the site of Melrose Clinic had been a private, psychiatric hospital for many years. In more recent times, it had modernised to offer mental health out-patient sessions and a specialised residential service for adolescents.

The atmosphere at Melrose Clinic seemed more like a hotel or spa retreat than a hospital. A casually-dressed receptionist showed Kal to a waiting lounge which smelled of coffee and chocolate and pastries. They were arranged in a mouth-watering display. Kal scooped up a chocolate brownie.

A large television screen played a popular nature series and two young people, who Kal thought were probably residents, played chess in the corner.

The furniture was of high quality, not resembling a student or adolescent residence, more like an exclusive club. Being cared for at a place like this must cost an absolute fortune. With everything supplied for Sophie – meals, cleaning, laundry, therapy and support – it would make it an incredibly difficult place to leave.

As soon as Kal set eyes on Sophie, she knew something had changed. Sophie's movements were slow, as if she dragged her arms and legs through treacle. It took her an age to cross the room.

Another young woman, dark haired and around the same age as Sophie, trailed Sophie across the floor. The second girl followed so closely it was almost as if the two of them were joined.

Kal felt a sinking feeling as she observed the second girl. She was so thin you could see her skull and bone structure as if her flesh had shrivelled. It reminded Kal of terrible photographs she'd seen of Holocaust survivors. Very likely this girl suffered from an eating disorder like anorexia and had done so for a long time. Her clothes were glitzy and fashionable but they hung ludicrously baggy. Kal found the overall effect shocking.

As the pair reached her, Kal saw a boy, younger than the two girls, slip in at the doorway. He took a seat over with the chess-players, who didn't give him a second glance.

'Oh Sophie, thank goodness I found you. I wish you hadn't run off without telling me.'

Kal wrapped her arms around Sophie. It was as if a layer of shine had been polished away, leaving Sophie dull. As well as being slow, the girl seemed listless.

'Kal. How did you find me?'

'Just a lucky guess and I was kinda surprised you came back to Melrose.'

Sophie sat next to Kal on the couch. The dark-haired girl remained standing, though she moved behind Sophie's far shoulder, maybe to remain as close to Sophie as possible whilst getting as much distance between her and Kal as she could.

126

'This is my friend, Eliza. She's shy so I don't think you should speak to her. We're best friends, like you and Marty I suppose.'

It was surprising Sophie's mind was clear enough to remember about Marty. Whatever medication Sophie was on, it must not have affected her thinking as much as it had had affected her physically.

'Eliza and I have known each other forever,' Sophie said, and Sophie took Eliza's hand.

The action was full of gentleness. Sophie really cared for Eliza. What must it have been like for these two? Dumped in this place, probably from an early age? Kal wanted to help them both so much, it started to hurt.

'You can sit down if you like, Eliza,' Kal said. 'I'm Sophie's friend, so I guess it makes me your friend too.'

Eliza made no sign she'd heard.

'The receptionist told me all this is voluntary, Sophie. She said you're free to come and go as you wish but your room is paid for all the time. How long have you been living here?'

Kal hoped Sophie hadn't been here since she was nine years old.

'After my parents died, my brother tried to look after me on his own. He hired a string of au pairs but it didn't work out and I was miserable all the time. I was sent to doctors and specialists. In the end, I went to boarding school and that didn't work out either because I had panic attacks. When I broke down, Dr Kaufman, who was an old friend of my father's, offered to look after me here. That was five years ago and I've been at Melrose ever since. Don't worry, it's a relief being here.

127

I've been studying for my diploma in Art and I want to train to be an art therapist. I had to postpone my application because of those terrible headaches I told you about.'

Sophie hadn't mentioned any headaches.

Kal glanced over to the television set. She wanted to keep it as relaxed and easy as possible, not like an interrogation. The boy over the other side of the room sat so he faced them and she knew he was watching everything and straining to catch every bit of their conversation.

'I'm not sure if you told me about getting headaches?'

'Yes, it's been the cause of all the trouble. I've been getting terrible headaches for the last few months. None of Dr Kaufman's medications seem to have much effect and he thought I should stall leaving here until we've sorted it out. It was a real shame because my new art teacher was really keen on helping me. He used to know my mother. He said I had a talent like hers.'

'Right, I see, well, I think I'd like to meet him. Only I thought you felt trapped here, Soph? Isn't that why you ran away?' Kal lowered her voice. There were no staff around, but in places like this, walls had ears.

'Gosh I'm so embarrassed about running from here in the rain and all that. It was a silly thing to do and I've no idea what came over me. Melrose is the best place for me.'

Kal stared at Sophie in astonishment. Not only were Sophie's words so different from those she'd said at Kal's apartment, her whole delivery and demeanour had transformed. The Sophie in front of Kal was compliant. That was the trouble with medication, it could change your whole mind state and personality, for the better or for the worse.

'Sophie should leave,' Eliza said. It was a whisper and the girl's voice was wheezy, as if she had trouble drawing strength to speak.

Kal saw Sophie squeeze Eliza's hand.

'I'm never going to leave you, Eliza, and we have to face the truth, I'm not a safe person to be around out there in the real world. I tried to stab you, didn't I Kal? It's better for me to be back here, where they can keep an eye on me.'

Kal's stomach flipped. Was Sophie saying she'd come back to Melrose to protect Kal? She'd given up her freedom because she'd attacked Kal?

'No, Sophie, no. I was never in danger from you.'

'We have to face the truth. I'm not a safe person to be around outside Melrose.'

Sophie repeated the same lines, her voice dull.

'Listen, Soph, I'm more than capable of looking after myself – you were never any threat. You left Melrose for a reason and I don't know what that reason was, only I know it was important. Important enough for you to be running into a road in the middle of a storm.'

She saw her words weren't getting through. A wall had been constructed and the Sophie she'd met in the rain could no longer be reached.

'Why don't you come back with me and we can try to piece it all together? You'll be safe at 701, I give you my word.'

'I can't,' Sophie said, and her tone sounded flat and final.

Kal's heart sank.

'Don't worry, I'm fine here. Besides, Eliza needs me and it was selfish of me to leave her. That's what friends are for, isn't it?'

Eliza stood quietly, so frail and ill-looking, as if she had no strength left and could collapse at any moment. It only confirmed to Kal how Sophie must have been desperate to get away if she'd been prepared to leave Eliza behind.

'Eliza's mother was a coke head. A millionaire one of course and she won't mind me telling you this, will you, Eliza? It's Eliza's birthday this weekend. She always hates it because Eliza found her mother dead from an overdose on her tenth birthday. Her father's a famous musician and he's off gigging on the other side of the world. So you see, I can't leave her on her own. I'd never do that.'

'I'm not going to try to persuade you, that wouldn't be fair.' Plus, Kal realised she had no chance of succeeding. 'I need to know if you're on any medication. Are they giving you anything new to take?'

If they were, Kal could investigate and get specialist advice, maybe find an alternative which wouldn't squash down Sophie's impulses.

'They're only giving me my usual sleeping pills. They help me to get off at night and it means I don't have nightmares.'

'What kind of nightmares?'

'Oh, I don't know. Stuff.'

'Can you give me one of the tablets?'

'If you want, but you don't need to do this, like I said, I'm fine here.'

Like hell you are, thought Kal. And Sophie hadn't even mentioned Purdy as if her cat didn't exist. Well-meaning or not, this place was taking something away from Sophie and it made Kal angry.

'The boy over the other side of the room has been watching ever since we came in. Is he a friend of yours?'

'That's Seb. He's in love with Eliza, and yes, he is, Eliza, don't try to deny it. He's harmless. Seb's always watching us and following Eliza everywhere she goes. He hardly ever says anything. You should see his room, he collects everything – bits of coloured paper, pretty stones, stamps, coins. Seb doesn't mean anything, he's just lonely. He doesn't get many visitors.'

Kal thought Seb probably heard every word and her eyes strayed to the boy. She figured him to be around fifteen, with a sensitive face and curly hair and an expression that was far too grim. She was glad Sophie didn't tell her Seb's story – she felt sure it would be terrible.

Kal wanted to take Sophie and Eliza with her. She wanted to scoop them up and march out and leave Melrose behind forever. Only she couldn't put them at risk like that. Kal realised there was something here they needed and, for once, she had to act responsibly.

'None of this feels right, Sophie, and if there's one thing I've learned in life, it's to trust my instincts. I'm going to get that pill tested and don't tell anyone about it and I'm going to come back tomorrow and every day and we'll talk much more, okay?'

No, none of this felt right and for all its comfort, she didn't like the feel of Melrose clinic.

Sophie smiled. 'You're nice, Kal, I thought it when we first met.'

'I wish I could take you away and help you sort out whatever's wrong. I know there's something.'

'I'm happy here, you don't need to worry. Why don't you come to Eliza' birthday? There'll be cake.'

'Of course I will,' Kal said, and when she gave Sophie a hug, Kal held on because she didn't want to let go.

Chapter Twenty-three

The summons filled her with dread.

Kal stared at the line of text from Dante Jones. Dante had been clear with Kal when she first made her request. A favour for a favour, that's how the Cartel operated. If the Baron helped Kal in her search for Alesha it left her in their debt.

'You bastard, Dante,' she said to herself. 'You've dumped me in a trap. I never asked you to go after Klaus.'

It stirred it all up again – about her father and the way he'd brainwashed her.

The criminal mind.

David Khan picked out seemingly ordinary people for their "projects".

He'd sent Kal to befriend them and analyse them. They made daily or weekly visits to the same innocent venues. She realised now how her father had carefully chosen their targets. They were all criminals. All deviant and twisted in their own ways. A paedophile canteen worker, a gambling newsagent hooked on blood sports, a neighbour who incarcerated his disabled wife and left her starving for days on end. David Khan kept sending her back until she'd unpicked them. And

praised her when she began to guess their secrets. It had been
a hard apprenticeship. And he'd been a severe taskmaster. Yes,
the criminal mind and the deviant mind were places she was
familiar with. In all their disguises.

As she made her way to Soho, Kal felt mixed up.
The feeling of dread wouldn't go away, even though a
meeting with Dante Jones from the Cartel didn't
frighten her. Her father had taken fear of criminality out
of her a long time ago. The bigger problem being he'd
replaced it with a thrill. The thrill of analysis. Of staring
into the face of evil and understanding the capacity of
the person in front of you. Kal recognised the feelings
inside her and in there was an anticipation at meeting
Dante again and the lure of being close to the edge. It
made her feel bad about herself.

Chinatown gave her its usual vibrant welcome. The
narrow streets were full of tourists and crowds. Locals
were going about their daily business. Scents from
Chinese restaurants filled the air. She passed eating
house windows with lines of ducks roasting on the spit,
the aromas spilling out. Men and women haggled and
talked loudly in English and in Mandarin. As Kal
turned the corner, she spotted a group of old men
playing dice at a restaurant table and she smiled. She
loved the vibe in this part of town.

A couple of streets down and Kal entered Soho.
Dante Jones kept his centre of operations in a burlesque
club. As on her first visit all those months ago, the same
smoothly dressed Peruvian security guard stood
outside. As before, the same waitress met Kal at the bar

and took her to the back room, knocking on Dante's door and then opening it for Kal to enter, and Kal walked into Dante's office. The Miro print still hung behind Dante's massive desk. Again she wondered if it was an original or a reproduction.

'How good of you to come so promptly,' Dante said.

'Hello, Dante.' *I didn't have much choice, did I?*

Dante bowed at the waist. He was tall and huge-shouldered and the bow was such a formal gesture that with most men it would've been ridiculous, and yet, with Dante, the effect was elegant. Kal recalled how he'd spoken warmly to her about a chance meeting with her father. As if Dante and her father had been a couple of normal people chatting in a bar, rather than two of the worst types of men she could imagine.

Dante was near the top of the pecking order. In the drugs world, the only person Dante would rely on was himself, though he'd hinted at the strength of the alliance between the Baron at the head of the drugs Cartel, and his favourites of which, apparently, David Khan had been one. Dante must have the confidence of the Baron too, to have been given their London operation to handle. That must say a lot for Dante's capacities for violence and strategy and Kal knew she must stay vigilant.

Dante led her past a full-sized pool table. An enormous leather chair groaned as he sat down.

'First, the Baron wanted you to know no intervention on our part could have changed events for your mother. However, given you and your father are so alike, the Baron decided to tidy up the loose ends for you.'

Klaus, she thought.

'Your father would never sanction leaving a man alive in such circumstances. We did it as a favour, so you didn't need to go after him yourself.'

Kal didn't want to speak. It was an unwise tactic when confronting an organisation as powerful as the Cartel. Better to play it as close and tight as possible and only respond to Dante's initiatives. Besides, she must never let them know how *unlike* she was to the Baron's favourite, David Khan. Nor how angry she felt at the Cartel's actions. She waited, cool and calm, listening to the sound of her own steady heartbeat.

'May I offer you a drink?' Dante asked.

'No, thank you.'

'I see you're ready to get down to business. I admire that – you really are very much like your father.'

It was to her advantage Dante knew only the superficial similarities between them – her training, her nerve, her skills.

The ice cubes tinkled in Dante's glass as he took a sip.

'The Baron has become quite interested in your talents. It's unusual for a young woman to be trained to such a high level and add to that you're based in London and you're a British citizen – you'd be an asset to any operation.'

'I'm a freelancer and I like it that way.'

'Yes, I'm sure you do, though one day you might realise the importance of protection and allegiance and the rewards for loyalty. Meanwhile, of course, there's the question of a small debt to be repaid.'

Oh god, just as she thought, they were manipulating her.

The Cartel's operation was huge. They organised the production of opium in a swathe of communes in Afghanistan, the manufacture of heroin in ramshackle laboratories hidden in the foothills of Pakistan, and then its global distribution to a system of middlemen and then dealers in Europe and America. Thanks to vast and hidden networks of organised crime, the Baron made billions a year.

The problem was she had very few options. If she objected now, this could turn nasty. Surely it would be better to repay them or make a semblance at it, and at the same time, get as much intelligence as she could on the Cartel and pass it to Spinks? Working as a mole from the inside seemed a much more attractive, and she had to admit, exciting prospect. In the space of a moment, she made a decision.

'I hope your proposition is going to be interesting,' she said, injecting boredom into her voice.

Dante's eyes glinted and Kal thought how a man like him had the temperament to strike with no mercy. Likely he kept a gun on him at all times and used it on those who displeased him, or who'd been dragged in front of him for crossing the Cartel. She wondered how many times he'd fired it in this office.

'What I mean is, I'm grateful and I'm looking forward to finding out how I can thank the Baron for his help.'

'No need to fawn with me, Kal, though some of our operatives like that type of behaviour. For instance, the Baron's son, Raphael. He's one who enjoys people pandering to his ego. In my experience, those who need that sort of reinforcement are hot and volatile. It makes them dangerous to work with.'

Though he'd wrapped up his comments, Kal's skin prickled. Dante was telling her private information about the Baron's family. Now why would he do that?

The Baron had two sons. The older one had been killed, and it was Kal's father who was sent to investigate and avenge that death. Raphael was the younger son.

'Your assignment will be with Raphael,' Dante said. 'I handle the London drug business and Raphael handles the Cartel's other activities. He'll brief you when you meet him. Whatever Raphael tells you to do, you do it. When the assignment is finished you'll be free of your obligations to us.'

So, it was as quick and simple as that. The Cartel wanted you to do something and you did it, no questions, no hesitation, no negotiation. The palms of her hands felt suddenly sweaty.

'I don't have a choice?'

'You always have choice, though if you refuse the project...' Dante spread his arms wide and shrugged.

What did that mean? If she refused they'd kill her? Or, more their style, they'd threaten someone she cared about until she complied?

'As I told you when we first met, never request a favour from the Baron unless you're willing to pay the price.'

'Can you give me more information? So I know what I'll be taking on?'

Dante sighed. 'Asking too many questions is never a good idea in our line of business.' He reached into his pocket and pulled out a packet of peppermints.

'Still trying to give up smoking?'

'I think of it as work in progress.'

Dante stared straight at Kal and she met his gaze.

What he saw in her eyes which made him change his mind, she couldn't guess.

'It's for Raphael to brief you on the job, not me,' he said, taking a couple of sweets. 'What I can tell you is Raphael was never his father's favourite. After his older brother's death, Raphael didn't let up on his father and used the Baron's grief to leverage a way into the business. Against his better judgement, the Baron allocated some of his older son's responsibilities, that's to say a large chunk of the Cartel's activities, to Raphael, though he would never agree to the boy taking on the drug operations. That's still a sore point with Raphael.'

The smell of mints wafted towards her.

'The biggest challenge for you will be managing Raphael's temperament. I suspect the job will be simple for someone with your expertise, though never forget, despite his inadequacies, Raphael is still the Baron's son. And his only son.'

'Right.'

'You'll meet Raphael and his minder Clarence, very soon. He'll be in touch.'

'Minder?'

'In this line of business, it's a good idea to have someone watching your back. Especially when you're an annoying little prick like Raphael.'

Dante stared at her again and downed the contents of his glass. He stood to escort Kal to the door.

She didn't push for more. She'd been lucky to get as much as she had. In fact, Dante had taken her by surprise with his revelations, meaning perhaps she really did remind Dante of her father. Maybe Dante's dislike of Raphael had played its part too.

At the door, he rested his hand lightly on her shoulder. It only landed there for a moment and was quickly gone as he leant to turn the door handle. It was a strange gesture for this man, a hardened professional. Kal's skin tingled. Dante would be one of the last people she'd expect to be protective. It left her puzzled and, strangely, slightly afraid.

Back on the street, Kal rubbed her arms to calm the goosebumps. She walked briskly back through Chinatown, though she couldn't enjoy the vibe this time.

Her adrenalin level slowly dropped. Why wouldn't her assignment be handled by Dante? Why leapfrog to the Baron's son? Surely Raphael would be higher up the hierarchy because of his blood-ties? And why had Dante given those warnings?

She must keep positive. Working with Raphael would give her the opportunity to find out more about how the Cartel operated and she couldn't deny part of her was curious to experience the world her father had inhabited.

Even better, it gave her a chance to damage the Cartel. She must let them think they were manipulating her, when all the time she would be manipulating them. It would be a dangerous game but she hated the Cartel and everything they stood for, so why not take her chance? And Spinks could profit from it. Yes, it was a great idea. This was going to be a challenge.

Chapter Twenty-four

As Kal checked the post box in the downstairs hallway, Mrs Robinson came hurrying out. Mrs Robinson's face told the story. Kal stuffed the letters into her pocket and her heart rate picked up.

'Oh, thank goodness you're back, my dear. I didn't know whether to call the police or what to do for the best.'

Kal placed a reassuring hand on the old woman's arm. 'What's happened?'

'That young girl you were asking about, Sophie, she came here. I saw her outside on the path and I went out, well, you said she was missing and I thought perhaps I could invite her in for a cup of tea. I knew something was terribly wrong as soon as I saw her. She was in a dreadful state. I could hardly make out what she was saying. I think she came looking for you but I couldn't calm her down. I'm so sorry dear, she refused to come inside.'

'Where did she go?'

'She started crying and ran off. Darn my arthritis. If only my grandson had been here I'd have sent him after her.'

'How long ago, Mrs Robinson, and did you see which way she went?'

'Oh I've been waiting and waiting for you to come back, Kal, but it wasn't that long ago, maybe almost an hour and she went down the path to the left, you know, towards the college?'

An hour. Sophie could get a long way in an hour.

Kal sprinted to the entrance, calling over her shoulder. 'Thank you so much, Mrs Robinson. I've got to find her.'

'Good luck my dear.'

She ran towards the shortcut which led through to the nearby college. It was a path trekked twice a day by local students. Pretty soon it would be full of teenagers spilling out of the college and chatting loudly and playing on their mobile phones. Sophie wouldn't know how much this path was used but wouldn't she avoid going towards the college, realising it would be busy at this time of day, perhaps with plenty of students hanging around the grounds? The college buildings were obvious.

Kal hesitated and swung off, heading around the back of the apartment building. The bin area lay on the far side and she wanted to do a quick check. Sophie would seek a refuge – somewhere to hide away from the crowds – somewhere dark and small. If Sophie had come looking for her, it might mean she'd try to stay as close as possible.

A row of large rectangular bins stood in a brick siding, sheltered by a low, sheet-metal roof. The area stank from the accumulation of gunge. The bins were on

143

wheels, and, as she'd done when she first searched this area, Kal examined the ground before she tried moving any of them. This time, she spotted a footprint in the mud. It was a small shoe size and of the right foot of a sneaker. The type of sneaker Sophie wore.

'Soph are you there? It's me, Kal.'

Silence.

'Are you there, Sophie? Everything's okay, please come out.'

Kal heard noises and then a scrape and one of the bins jerked a little. From behind, Sophie crawled out on her hands and knees, her jeans and jacket filthy, her eyes desperate. Kal dropped down and put her arms around the girl, pulling her close. Sophie was freezing cold and her muscles were rigid.

'Eliza,' Sophie whispered.

Kal's heart missed a beat.

Sophie's mouth moved again. 'Eliza's dead.'

Chapter Twenty-five

It took a lot to shake Kal. The death of such a delicate girl as Eliza felt like one of the great injustices of the world. Eliza deserved a good life. She deserved a long life, leaving behind the troubles of her family. And how she deeply regretted not taking them both with her when she left Melrose. Kal sat with Sophie while Sophie curled in a ball, rocking and moaning.

For almost an hour, they stayed that way. Kal thought about Sophie's short life, and Eliza's, and how much misery and suffering had been stuffed into both of them. It made her feel sick inside, and determined and ruthless. She waited, watching the sun sink towards the horizon.

Only when the sobbing stopped did the story start to come, spurting out between bouts of shaking. It took time to make sense of it all.

Eliza had been found dead in her bed earlier that day – the morning of her eighteenth birthday. It was Sophie who discovered her, and although the nurses at Melrose and emergency services had done everything they could to resuscitate her, Eliza was reported dead on arrival at accident and emergency.

A suicide note had been found. According to the word doing the rounds at Melrose, Eliza had overdosed on prescription medication. Melrose had rigorous procedures and an investigation was already underway to find out how a vulnerable girl might have access to restricted and strictly supervised substances.

As Kal pieced together the information, she felt a growing sense of unease.

'Tell me again, although Eliza dreaded her birthdays, you thought she was in a positive frame of mind when you left her last night?'

'It doesn't make sense. If she was going to kill herself I would've realised something was wrong. When Eliza's been depressed or hurting in the past, sometimes I sleep in her room even though it's not allowed, and the nurses turn a blind eye. I was ready to do it last night, only it didn't seem she needed me. If anything, she seemed more positive than usual, like she had something to look forward to.'

'Did anything different happen during the day?'

'Her family lawyer visited. It's a woman and I've seen her before. She comes every six months to talk about finance and plans and stuff like that. She's quite nice and I suppose she wanted to let Eliza know what would happen for the coming year, you know, whether she would stay at Melrose and all.'

'And?'

'And nothing. Of course she was staying.'

It all sounded so straightforward. A vulnerable girl who dreaded her birthdays, who took her own life because she couldn't bear to continue as she was. That's why Kal didn't buy the scenario. Especially since Sophie had been ready to stay with Eliza. Kal had seen how close the two of them were, and she knew first-hand how astute Sophie was. Sophie would've known if something was wrong and she would've stayed close to comfort Eliza and prevent a tragedy.

'Did she try to take her life before?'

Sophie hesitated. 'Yes, but it was different. She was in a bad patch.'

'I'm glad you came to find me, Soph.'

'So am I. You're solid. Like people can lean on you and you won't break.'

Kal gave Sophie a sharp look. 'Is that why you came back?'

Again, Sophie hesitated. 'Yes.'

At that moment, Purdy decided to make an entrance. She strutted across the lounge floor and jumped onto Sophie's lap.

'I knew you'd be a great cat-sitter.'

Kal was glad she'd remembered to put food out that morning. The poor animal had acted half starved.

Standing up, she walked over to the window and stared at the trees running all the way along the side of Wimbledon Common. She kept her back to Sophie. Two joggers were heading this way, their running shoes bright against the grey pavement.

The girl was withholding something. Likely a key piece of information. Certainly linked to Eliza's death. And Sophie seemed to have snapped right out of her lethargic state. The shock could have done that. Kal was still waiting for the results of the pill analysis but was

Sophie implicated here? Had she any part in Eliza's death? No, she didn't think so. If she pushed and forced to get that last piece of information out of her, it would likely destroy any bond they had between them. Half-closing her eyes, she listened to her gut instinct. *Wait*, said the voice in her head, *let the confession come in its own time*, and so she turned around and gave Sophie a sad smile.

'Penny's been killed and now Eliza. I don't think this is over yet and you'd better stick with me until it is.'

Sophie nodded and curled up with the cat. Her face was puffed up from all the crying and Kal saw again the girl's resilience. Sophie had strength of character. What a horrible, gruesome discovery to find your best friend dead. She felt even more certain that deep down inside, Sophie had more reserves than she realised. Kal stroked Purdy and tucked the cushion more comfortably behind Sophie's head.

Thanks to her summoning by Dante, Kal had missed the planning meeting for Marty's homecoming but there was no way she was going to miss the actual event. The best place for Sophie would be by her side. Or if that wasn't possible, by Marty's side, and Marty's homecoming would be a great opportunity for the two of them to meet. She watched while Sophie fell asleep. Then she tip-toed out of the lounge.

***

The knee held out for the workout and Kal made sure not to over-stress it.

She'd missed her usual kung fu sessions. Whenever she stayed in London she'd the habit of attending her old club and normally, she'd have been going down there at least three times a week to clear her head and burn off the stress. Kal flexed her knee. It was pride too that kept her away, because she didn't want LeeMing to see her not at her best. That was stupid and she knew it.

After going through a full routine of stretching and power exercises, Kal sat for a long meditation. When she finished, she opened her eyes to find Sophie standing in the doorway, staring at her.

'I wasn't spying, I wondered what you were doing,' Sophie said quickly.

'Being curious isn't spying, Sophie, you didn't do anything wrong.' Kal patted the mat beside her. 'Come and sit with me. I've been doing martial arts since I was a kid and meditation is a key part of the discipline – it allows me to let go of distractions and keep focused.'

'I bet you're pretty good at martial arts. You look the type.'

'Do I?'

People didn't usually say that because she preferred to hide her abilities. Often, she hid them simply by wearing very girly clothes. It wasn't always wise to show your strengths – a better strategy was to keep them as a surprise, especially in uncertain or dangerous situations. She patted the mat again, avoiding filling Sophie in on her level of skill.

'Will you teach me?' Sophie asked.

'What? Meditation or martial arts?'

'Both.'

Sophie was serious.

'It takes years to become proficient. I've got to say it could really help you with your confidence and with your emotions. Most people learn it for self-defence but it has much more to offer.'

'My half-brother, Raymond, would probably like it then. He's always telling me I've got a problem with self-esteem.'

'I didn't put it that way.'

'I know. I guess Raymond's not as diplomatic as you. I'm just one big problem he'd like to get rid of.'

What must it have been like losing your parents and being left with a selfish, greedy shit like Raymond? Pretty dreadful, she imagined.

'Ever since Mum and Dad died he's tried to suffocate me. He's the one who put me in Melrose. He's the one who signed the papers so he doesn't have anything to do with me. When I first went there I was drugged up to the eyeballs and it was his doing.'

Sophie didn't hide the bitterness.

'Penny was my only friend and Raymond always hated her.'

'Why would he feel like that?'

'Why do you think? Because Penny was a prostitute and runs a brothel of course. Raymond hated her, and he hated how Penny wanted me to get out of Melrose and build my own life. But she was the only one who cared about me.'

'You told me she and your mum were friends?'

'Yes, I've known her all my life.'

'Right, well maybe Raymond was worried about you. You've got money, maybe he thought Penny was trying to manipulate you?'

'Bullshit. Raymond is the one who manipulates. Always dragging me back to Melrose when I tried to get away. Penny cared about me and she didn't give a damn about my money.'

Again, Kal regretted not meeting Penny so she could've made her own assessment. A clever manipulator can always make it seem they care for you. It's one of their best tricks and works so well on the lonely and desperate. Once they've got their claws in, a victim doesn't find the strength to get away because they're too reliant on the affection.

Sophie was struggling to keep her emotions in. Tears started to flow.

'This is what we're going to do. First I'm going to talk you through a guided meditation. Then, you're going to rest and sleep if you can. Tomorrow I'd like you to meet Marty. I know going outside is the last thing you want to do but I'm going to be right there with you. Are you willing to try?'

'They covered Eliza's lovely face with a sheet and when I saw them wheeling her away something inside me broke. I wanted to fall on the floor and never get up. They left me in a chair in the corner. The police questioned me and then the nurses put me to bed. It was all I could do to crawl back here.'

'I'm so sorry, Sophie. I can't imagine how horrible it must have been.'

Sophie made gulping sounds. 'Whatever you've got inside that makes you strong, I want it. I don't want to be weak anymore. I want to fight. For Eliza. I want to find out who did this.'

And Kal could see she was telling the truth.

Chapter Twenty-six

'Hello Detective Inspector.'

'Actually, as of last month, it's Detective Chief Inspector.'

'Congratulations Detective Chief Inspector. Do you meet all your clandestine contacts at close to midnight, or is it only me?'

'You're not a clandestine contact Ms Medi, but yes, I rather like this little bench for our meetings, don't you? And my promotion made it a bit easier to get hold of the autopsy report on Penelope Sanders. We found traces of date rape drug in her bloodstream. Cause of death – blood loss from the laceration across her abdomen. The cutting away of the eyelids occurred before death.'

He glanced at her to check he wasn't being too blunt with the details.

'Hey, you know me better than that. Go ahead.'

'The national database threw up five unsolved murders where the eyelids of the victims had been removed. Four of them were young women believed to be prostitutes. The murders have an interesting geographical spread and a curious time pattern. I can let you have access to the files and you'll see the signature on the killings is the same. The bodies have the same injuries and the killer arranges the victim's hair in the same way, like a fan, and they take time to brush and put on lacquer to keep it that way.'

The same as she'd seen with Penny.

'No evidence to link the crimes?'

'Police questioned a number of suspects and no charges were brought. I hope to make headway with the death of Ms Saunders and then I can see if any links can be made.'

Kal nodded. 'I think you should bring two other deaths into the picture. Seven years ago, Charlotte and Martin Kendrick were murdered and something tells me there's a connection. It's not the same modus operandi but I'd like to know if Charlotte got any of the same treatment.'

Down the path, a late-night jogger was approaching and he gave the two of them a strange look. She supposed he might wonder about a young woman meeting a much older man. Kal gave the jogger an evil glare and the man speeded up.

Spinks cleared his throat. 'Let's not frighten the locals, Ms Medi.'

She gave him her most innocent look.

'The lab tested the pills you gave me. They're placebos,' he said.

That was a shock. 'Are you sure?'

Spinks didn't stoop to answer.

'I was expecting some kind of mind-altering drug. Something heavy.'

If Sophie wasn't being manipulated by drugs, then what the hell was happening to her?

Though Kal was sure he didn't have enough light to read it, Spinks glanced at his watch.

'Let's keep in contact on this one,' he said. 'I have another meeting I need to attend.'

'At quarter to midnight?'

'Oh yes. And the park will be closing soon. You'd better make sure you don't get locked inside.'

She nodded and then he went one way and she another.

She had plenty to think about and none of it was making any sense.

***

After an analysis of Spinks' files, Kal pushed back from the keyboard. In here was a pattern. It showed the trail of a killer addicted to killing and she was certain it was one person. But this was a serial killer who'd strayed from their normal pattern more than once, and that was unusual.

A first kill often had discrepancies because the perpetrator was learning their craft. People had been caught that way years down the line due to early slip-ups. Often the first victim was chosen from the local area, or from within the network of the killer. In this case, it explained why the first victim was not a prostitute.

Then the killer had adjusted their aim and targeted sex workers.

The time line was another interesting factor. All the deaths occurred before Charlotte Kendrick. Then came a long period of quiet which had been broken by the death of Penny Saunders. What had been the trigger to make the killer return to old habits? What had kept them quiet in the meantime?

And what about the arrangement of the victims' hair? It must hold a significance for the killer. They wanted the victim to look a certain way. Was it a display like a peacock's fan to show off the killer's work? Or was it symbolic?

Kal threw Eliza's death into the mix. She didn't believe in coincidences which meant the young girl had been killed for a reason. Though it was a death outside the killer's pattern, Kal felt sure she was staring at one killer and one profile.

Find what held it all together and she'd nail them. And it all kept circling back to Sophie.

Kal downed her peppermint tea, long since gone cold. The only certainty she felt was the killer would strike again. They were back on a spree, and she was pretty certain there wouldn't be a year between the deaths this time. No, things had speeded up and it was only a matter of time before they took another victim, most likely a prostitute. She sent Spinks a text to warn him.

Chapter Twenty-seven

'You should've told me about poor Eliza and I would've cancelled the damn party. It wasn't my idea in the first place,' Marty said.

Marty and Kal were in the kitchen at Marty's apartment. Through the doorway, Marty could see Sophie hunched at a table. The other guests were in a light mood, chatting and laughing, and it made Marty feel extra bad for what the girl must be going through.

'Sophie's had the night to get over the worst of the shock. She needs time to come to terms with it,' Kal said.

'It's going to take a bunch of time to come to terms with another of her friends being murdered.'

'Eliza's suicide note must've been faked, I'm convinced of it. I'm going to get Spinks involved.'

'And meanwhile I hope we're going to do some digging of our own,' Marty said. 'I can see from your face you've been planning the next move.'

'Of course I have,' Kal said, staring at an attractive woman on the far side of the lounge. She had auburn hair swept up into a pony tail and she had long legs. Yes, of course she had. Kal tried not to grit her teeth.

'I thought you'd clock LeeMing's girlfriend. Her name's Fiona,' Marty said. 'Attractive, isn't she?'

'I'm not clocking anyone.'

Marty watched as her brother gave LeeMing a friendly slap on the shoulder. It was good to see the people she cared about in the swing of their own lives rather than sitting fretting at her bedside.

'You're not going to like this, Kal, but there's one question I've got. If Eliza's death wasn't suicide who supplied the pills? I mean, it was an overdose, so if it was voluntary or if it was forced, someone had access to restricted substances. Eliza got the supply from someone or somewhere.'

Kal didn't say anything.

Marty was careful to keep her voice even. 'And did Sophie had access? What if Sophie hoarded her own supply of medication? Did you think about it?'

'Only briefly. Believe me, it's a non-runner.'

Marty crossed her arms. 'From an outside point of view, Sophie is the only link between the two killings. Fact – she was the first to discover Eliza. Fact – something happened at Montgomery Road, we don't know what, and she hid in the laundry basket. What if Sophie was upstairs with Penny? I mean, the girl attacked you with a knife, we can't dismiss that.'

'She's been traumatised. Sophie gets re-triggered and then she can't remember what happened or what's she's been doing.'

'My point exactly. And you said she changed. When she attacked you she'd gone into a dark frame of mind like it wasn't really her.'

'Sophie isn't a killer.'

'You told me yourself you saw hatred in her eyes.'

'And?'

Marty could see Kal getting more and more defensive and annoyed. Better back off for now or she risked her friend walking out on her. Besides, if Sophie posed a risk to Kal, Marty intended to be around. The last thing she wanted was Kal cutting her out.

Marty took a sip of apple juice. 'All I'm saying is, let's keep it in mind.'

'Sure, and I think I'd better go and check on her right now.'

Marty watched as Kal fussed around Sophie, offering crisps and another drink, even though the girl was lost in her own world, unaware of activity around her, her eyes unfocused. Why would Kal change from someone who didn't give a second glance to strays of any kind? What was it about this girl that had got to Kal? Whatever it was, it worried Marty. Kal's judgement was off. And that was bad.

As Kal walked around the table, she moved awkwardly. Marty stared. Kal injured her leg in India in a near-death incident and it looked like the knee was still giving problems. That wasn't good news either. And definitely not something Kal would want to talk about. She made a mental note never to mention it. Then, as Fiona made directly for Kal, Marty bolted out of the kitchen. She wondered wryly how many guests had been beaten to death at homecoming parties.

'LeeMing told me all about you,' Fiona said. 'Sounds like you're a bit of a power woman.'

'Oh yeah?' Kal said.

'Hi, Marty. Great to see you again.' Fiona was all smiles.

Marty caught Kal's accusing look.

'You're looking much stronger already,' Fiona said.

'Thanks,' Marty replied, really wishing she'd warned Kal about Fiona's job.

'You two have met then?' Kal said.

'Of course, we've met loads of time.' Fiona was completely missing the barb in Kal's comments. 'I'm a physiotherapist at the hospital, didn't Lee tell you? And I hope you don't mind but I kinda noticed you still seem a bit stiff in your leg. I guess it's from the thing that happened in India?'

Marty had a sinking feeling in her stomach.

'I'd be happy to suggest some exercises if you'd like to-'

'No, I wouldn't.'

Kal's rudeness cut the conversation dead and Fiona stifled a nervous laugh.

'Oh, don't mind my friend,' Marty said, 'directness is her middle name.' And she took Kal's elbow and steered her away.

'I didn't know you two were such good buddies.'

Kal sounded calm but Marty knew better. One of her friend's worst traits was jealousy.

'Fiona's been one of my therapists and she's great. I should've given you the heads up on that one only I got distracted by…' Marty jerked her head towards Sophie and turned to look. 'Shit.'

The girl sat rigid in her chair, her eyes were screwed shut and her hands were fists pressed at her temples. She looked like she was about to have a fit.

And Sophie did. She toppled sideways, landing with a thud. Then she started screaming and kicking.

A wave of weakness came over Marty and she leant on the back of a chair. The others were quickly by Sophie's side. Kal, Fiona, Marty's mother, LeeMing – there was plenty of help on hand. Marty got her breath back, glad the others hadn't noticed her sudden fatigue. Working with Kal was intense and getting to the bottom of the murders was demanding. Marty realised she wasn't quite up to it and she really, really wanted to be.

Kal's arms were around Sophie and she'd stopped thrashing. The girl was trying to speak.

'Penny – dead.'

'I know, Sophie,' Kal said, 'I'm so sorry, Penny's dead.'

Sophie shook her head. 'Penny – dead.'

Marty knelt opposite Kal and their eyes briefly met.

Sophie said, 'I – saw – him.'

Chapter Twenty-eight

'I – saw – him. It was Sugar G.'

'Sugar G?' Kal said, glancing up at Marty.

They manhandled Sophie into the kitchen and propped her against the cabinets. Marty closed the door.

'Tell us from the beginning,' Kal said, 'and go slowly.'

'Sitting at the table it all came back to me. I remember I wanted to ask Penny something and I went upstairs. I found her lying on the bed with blood... and her eyelids, I mean her eyes were... it was horrible... I tried to wake her up. I shouted and I shook her and her head flopped.' Sophie put her hands to cover her face.

'I know it was horrific. The poor woman had been brutalised,' Kal said. She made herself pause and not crowd in with questions.

'While I was bending over Penny, someone came out of the bathroom. It was Sugar G.'

Kal did a double take. 'Are you sure? Did he have anything in his hands? Was there any, you know, blood on him?'

'Not that I remember. He stared right at me but it was like he didn't really see me. He looked so angry. Then he ran out the room.'

'Did he say anything? Did Sugar G threaten you?'

'No nothing. He didn't say a word.'

'And the next thing you remember you were at Kal's flat?' asked Marty.

Sophie nodded. 'Why did I blank that out? I don't understand.'

'You found your friend murdered in a grotesque way. Your mind made you forget it to protect yourself,' Kal said.

'It makes Sugar G the main suspect,' Marty said. 'He's placed at the scene. He had access. Privacy. What about motive?'

Sophie shook her head. 'That doesn't make sense. Sugar G adored Penny. He'd do anything for her, literally, and if my reading of Penny's right, she felt the same way about him. Though they kept their relationship secret, I'm certain I'm right.'

'What?' said Kal. 'Sugar G and Penny had a thing going on? You're kidding me.'

'Why shouldn't they have? They've known each other since forever. I think they were in love,' Sophie said.

Marty frowned. 'He was a spurned lover then. Someone else came on the scene and got between them and Sugar G lost the plot.'

'What happened to Penny isn't the modus operandi of a jilted lover,' Kal said. 'That's the MO of a sociopath.'

***

Kal and Sophie got dropped back at 701 and Sophie sat on the settee cradling a mug of hot chocolate.

'Why are you helping me, Kal?'

'Because you've lost your two dearest friends. Because you need someone on your side.'

'No. Why are you really helping me?'

Kal stroked Purdy and thought about David Khan's last act of butchering leaving behind a child like Sophie. A child who was probably plagued by post-traumatic stress disorder the same as Sophie. Who likely struggled to lead an ordinary life. Who would forever be left with the scars of her father's violence and brutality. Kal shivered. She preferred to shoulder the shame alone. Besides, would saying it aloud make any difference?

'This is the second chocolate you've made for me since we got back from Marty's,' Sophie said. 'She really cares about you but I guess you know that already. She's got a strong spirit, hasn't she?' Sophie took a sip of chocolate. 'Are you going to answer my question?'

Kal cleared her throat. 'It's to do with my father. He was a nasty man. I feel I need to make up for all his...' She searched for the right word - Violence? Killings? Murders? – none of them seemed right.

'Oh,' Sophie said. 'You never mentioned your father before.'

No, thought Kal, and neither would you if you knew anything about him. She shrugged. 'It's complicated.'

'Something tells me you're ashamed of him. Don't worry, it can't be that bad. You're far too nice. Oh, and I shouldn't have eavesdropped I know, except I heard

Marty asking about me. She thinks Eliza's death has something to do with me, doesn't she? I don't blame her. I suppose you told Marty I'm a head case and you wouldn't be wrong. Maybe she thinks it's me who supplied the drugs?'

'Marty doesn't know you as well as I do.'

'Of course she doesn't. Thing is, she's right.'

Sophie's almond eyes stared straight at Kal and Kal went very still and concentrated. She'd locked Sophie's knife away but it would have been easy for Sophie to have picked up another along the way.

'Marty's right, Eliza's death was my fault.'

'Soph-'

'Hear me out. I told you Eliza's lawyer visited before her birthday. That's because we had a plan. It was our secret. Eliza and I planned to move out of Melrose. As soon as I got my money we were going to buy our own place. Eliza's lawyer was going to help us. That's why Eliza was killed – because of our secret plan to escape.'

Kal could see the torment. The girls had planned to be free and Sophie firmly believed this was responsible for Eliza's death. It was the piece of the puzzle she had sensed Sophie withheld.

She took hold of Sophie's hand. 'You cared for Eliza and it's not your fault. I know it and you know it. I believe in you, Sophie. It doesn't matter what Marty or anyone else thinks. You are innocent and whoever killed Eliza is a monster. And clever. And I promise you, I'm going to nail them.'

Chapter Twenty-nine

'Her name was Isabella Landry. She's twice been cautioned for soliciting,' Spinks said. 'You were right. The killer's started another spree.'

It was a dingy room in a run-down area, full of dark furniture and smelling of death and blood and incense. Spinks had called her to the crime scene and the killer had struck in the north of London which meant they were likely based in the metropolis. And they'd not had the time or the patience to plan this one.

'The urge to kill was too strong,' she said. 'They couldn't wait. Killing Penny has started them off again.'

'Agreed.'

The pathologist had already filled them in on her findings. Isabella Landry died from blood loss and her eyelids had been removed prior to death.

Kal stared down at Isabella. Her hair streamed out in the same arrangement.

'Any ideas what this is supposed to say?' she said.

'Your guess is as good as mine. It means something to the killer, but you'd have to be inside their mind to know what.'

'Hmmm, the idea of a halo keeps coming up for me. Have there been any other religious references?'

'None that we found. No messages and no significant locations for the murders, but I can get my team to check back. Oh yes, and I pulled in the information on the Kendrick murders. The pathologist described Charlotte's killing as a crime of passion. She was stabbed multiple times in the chest and stomach areas. There wasn't the cutting away of the abdomen and her eyelids were intact, but the link was there – her hair was arranged after she died.'

'Into the fan?'

'You got it.'

Shit. The answers were swimming around in the soup of intel. But she couldn't quite grasp them, couldn't quite worm her way deeper into this perpetrator's mind. But she knew she was very close.

Kal took another tour of the body, taking in the details. Isabella had died on the bed, the same as Penny. On a bedside table, was a half-burned stick of incense and a yellow china cat, the type you could buy in Chinese shops that was supposed to bring you good luck. Kal gritted her teeth. It hadn't brought Isabella good luck tonight. She tried not to think about the woman's last moments, staring up into the face of her killer.

Spinks was giving her an odd look. Right. He must have joined up the dots. The room was small, cramped even, it must have been where Isabella saw her clients. Spinks stuck right behind her as she toured the room.

'The name Kendrick has come up in connection with an incident at a private clinic. A young girl was found dead,' he said.

Spinks stared at Kal and she didn't give anything away. Did Spinks trust her? She'd soon find out.

'They're searching for a young girl to bring in for questioning; a Sophie Kendrick.'

'Oh?'

Spinks' body posture remained calm. He was assessing her and deciding what to say.

'Is she a suspect?' Kal asked.

'A supply of medication was found in Sophie Kendrick's room. The same type on which the girl, Eliza, overdosed. Ms Kendrick needs to answer questions. You should be aware Ms Kendrick is unstable and believed to be a danger to herself and others. Apparently, Sophie Kendrick attacked Eliza in the past – she knifed Eliza in the stomach.'

Spinks was no fool. He'd remember Sophie as the girl Kal brought to the riverbank. How much slack would he be prepared to cut her?

'Sounds to me as if someone might be trying to frame her,' Kal said.

'Are you sure about that?'

The lamps set up by the crime team accentuated his hooded eyes. Spinks seemed every inch the experienced detective he was. Kal could sense his ease with this conversation. She hoped it signalled his ease with her. If Kal didn't know herself better she'd say she was actually starting to like him.

'A misjudgement at this stage would be very serious,' he said. '*Every* suspect must be treated with equal consideration.'

'Yeah, I know. And with all that stabbing, it might make someone think Sophie Kendrick killed her own mother, even though she was only nine years old at the time?'

The team were preparing to transport the body and the two of them exited to the hallway to make more space.

'It's a possibility, however remote. I hope for Ms Kendrick's sake she presents herself to a police station within, say, the next twenty-four hours. And it goes without saying anyone she might be with must stay extra alert for their own safety.'

Message received, DCI Spinks.

She nodded. 'This is a clever bastard, DCI Spinks, and not a child. Let's get to work.'

Chapter Thirty

Arthur Connell lived in the suburbs. With a trimmed hedge and rose bushes along the path, the semi-detached house sat tidy and neat. According to Sophie, Connell had been her art tutor for less than a year. Sophie's previous teacher, widowed and approaching retirement, had found a new partner in life and jetted off. Arthur Connell had stepped in to take her place.

Kal rang the bell for the second time. She blocked out how the more Sophie fidgeted, the more Marty frowned. Marty hadn't wanted to bring Sophie along, saying Sophie wasn't able to deal with this sort of pressure, but Kal understood Connell's arrival at Melrose coincided with the onset of Sophie's headaches and she intended to find out why. Having Sophie in the room was essential and it would give Kal more space to dig around. Marty would have to shelve it.

'You sure it's the right address?' Marty asked.

'Mr Connell's probably absorbed in drawing. He gets distracted and forgets what he's supposed to be doing,' Sophie said.

'I sent him a message saying we were on our way,' Kal said.

She was about to give the door a good thudding, when it opened.

Late fifties, with grey hair tied in a ponytail, Connell looked the artistic type. He had vague, dreamy eyes and a slight squint. He wore grey trousers and a pink, crumpled shirt with the sleeves rolled up and one of them rolled way higher than the other. His blue, fluffy slippers seemed out of place. Connell gave Kal a smile and held out his hand.

'Goodness, you got here sooner than I expected,' Connell said, pushing his glasses up his nose. 'Welcome, please come in.' He ushered the three of them into the hallway. 'What a terrible time this is and such dreadful news about poor Eliza. My dear Sophie, I'm so sorry.'

Connell patted Sophie on the back in a kind way, and Sophie gave a little nod and gulped, prompting Marty to give Kal a look of death. Kal pretended not to notice. On his way into the lounge, Connell shooed away a cat but it slipped around his legs to jump onto the settee.

'Please take a seat and I hope you don't mind animals? I must say I was a little surprised by your phone call, Ms Medi, how can I help?'

'Thanks for making time to see us, Mr Connell,' Kal said. 'As I explained, I'm a friend of Sophie's and I'm helping her investigate her family tree. I'm sure you can appreciate how important it is for Sophie to understand as much as she can about her family and it's a cathartic project too, to come to terms with who she is and where she comes from. It's ongoing work and we decided to press on with it, despite recent – you know – events.'

'Yes, yes of course. Sometimes it's best to keep activities going, otherwise the mind simply dwells and slides into melancholy. Though I imagine Raymond would be the best person to ask about family matters.'

'Brother-sister relationships aren't always straightforward, Mr Connell,' Kal said.

She gave him a smile, which he returned. Connell seemed a straightforward, gentle man. Good manners, middle class tastes in furniture and decoration. There were no photographs of family in the lounge and no sign of a Mrs Connell or a partner, though the room appeared homely. Kal wondered where Connell kept his art work – perhaps he'd converted one of the rooms into a studio.

The cat moved to sit in between Marty and Sophie and it turned its back on Marty and started rubbing its face on Sophie's leg. Kal noticed it only had one eye. That was unusual for a cat and she wondered how it had lost it. She gave Sophie a nod and a smile of encouragement.

'You knew Mum, didn't you Mr Connell? I remember you mentioning it when we first met,' Sophie said.

Connell nodded. 'Your mother and I were at art college together. Dr Kaufman told me not to talk to you about Charlotte and I admit I found his advice a bit silly. Still, a job at a place like Melrose Clinic isn't an opportunity that comes around very often, so I agreed. After all, he's the expert and I didn't want to upset you.'

'Would you be willing to talk about Sophie's mother here in private? It's all confidential,' Kal said.

'Please Mr Connell, I know so little about my Mum,' Sophie said. 'And I worry one day I won't remember anything about her at all.'

Connell's glasses had slipped down his nose and he looked directly at Kal as he pushed them up. Someone less observant would have missed it. Or might have dismissed it as a trick of the light. Not Kal. She knew what she'd seen. Connell's eyes hadn't changed focus as they adjusted to his thick rimmed glasses. Now he looked at Kal from behind them and she kept her mouth in a gentle smile but she hadn't been fooled. Those glasses were made of plain glass, she was sure of it. Which meant Connell didn't wear them for his eyesight. Why would someone pretend to need glasses? Kal felt herself go calm inside. Calm and icy. Connell was not what he seemed. He wore glasses to steer people off track, to create a distraction. He liked to display himself as a weaker person, a bit of a scatter brain, a dreamer, and yet, his trick with the glasses meant Connell had a side he kept away from public view. A secret side, cunningly concealed under a front of absent-mindedness. Her skin prickled.

Connell sighed. 'When I knew her, Charlotte Kendrick was a beautiful young woman. So talented, and carefree, you know, someone with a wistful quality about them, with her head in the clouds. I was an impressionable young man and I thought she was wonderful. I think a lot of the students in our circle were a little bit in love with her. Oh, don't get me wrong, it was nothing serious, I'm only trying to explain how magnetic she was. When Charlotte agreed to marry your father, Sophie, there were plenty of disappointed admirers.'

'Did you know Martin Kendrick too?' asked Marty.

'Not really, he was a lot older than us. About twelve years her senior, I think, and an ambitious man in the medical field.'

Connell appeared to be telling the truth. Kal kept her concentration steady and focused, alert for any more giveaways.

'Can you tell us something about Charlotte's background? Did you ever meet her family?' Kal said.

'We'd all left home to follow our dreams of life as an artist. Few people talked about their home lives, certainly not Charlotte. We were a group of young people having fun, studying art and throwing all our passion into it.'

'What about her interests outside of college?'

'I've no idea. I think I have some photographs I can show you, if it might help?'

Yes, he was quite an artist, and she didn't mean at painting. Connell had skimmed onto the photographs like an expert manipulator. Brushing over the questions about Charlotte and suggesting an offering of photographs which Sophie would find it hard to resist. Kal didn't rush to accept what she knew to be a distraction. Why had he skimmed? Either he knew nothing about Charlotte, or he knew something significant he didn't want to tell, and Kal felt clear which of those she'd put her money on. Kal watched

Connell's left hand as he raised it and shifted his glasses up the bridge of his nose.

'Still there must've been times you shared stories? You must have known something about Charlotte outside of your lives at college?'

Connell pressed his lips together. 'Absolutely not. We were a close-knit group and we socialised together. As far as I know, no one was interested in doing things outside of our circle because we had so much in common.'

'Right.'

He was lying. She could see it in the restriction of his shoulders. In the way the muscles had tightened around his mouth. A sudden thought popped into Kal's mind – of course, Charlotte had been a sex worker. It didn't fit with her wealthy image but so what? It was the only explanation which made sense. That's why she and Penny were friends. That's how she fitted in with the pattern of killings. And she'd bet her money Arthur Connell knew.

Kal glanced over to the settee and Marty picked up the cue.

'If you have photos that'd be lovely,' Marty said.

'Hang on a moment and I'll dig them out.'

Connell was half way out the room when Kal went after him. She had a sudden desire to see his artwork. 'What kind of art do you like to do?' she asked.

His expression flickered. He was surprised. And not pleased.

'With the students, I concentrate on their portfolio for application to college. In Sophie's case, she's been working on sketches, portraits, landscapes and watercolours. Watercolours are her favourites. To be an art therapist, she needs to gain an art degree first and then study art therapy as a specialised discipline. It's a demanding path.'

'I see.' That was a neat side-step too. Though he offered plenty of information, designed to entice her interest, Connell told her nothing about his own work.

They'd reached the kitchen. At the back of the property, an added-on conservatory served as a studio. Through the sliding patio doors, she could see Connell's work on an easel. The painting was a stark, grey image of a hooded figure standing in an open field. The figure's face was partly hidden by the hood but what you could see of it was more skull than face. Bits of the body were missing and the landscape showed through the spaces. It looked like a rider of the apocalypse. Connell's eyes followed Kal's gaze.

He gave a tight smile. 'Do you like it?'

'Er, well, it grabs the attention.'

The kitchen had a pine table with two wooden benches, one of the benches neatly designed to fit around the corner of the room. Connell opened up the seat of that one. Over his shoulder, Kal saw it contained a storage of cardboard shoe boxes, some twenty in all. He selected one and his fingers didn't hesitate, even though the boxes didn't seem to be labelled. So, Connell knew exactly which box contained pictures of Charlotte? Why would that be? It meant this wasn't an old storage area – it was somewhere Connell delved into regularly. Kal made sure not to show too much interest.

She followed him back to the lounge, feeling the eyes of the hooded figure boring into her back.

Placing the box on the coffee table, Connell brought out a bunch of photographs and they all gathered round. The pictures showed a group of young people in a bar. Charlotte stood out immediately. First of all because she looked like Sophie, and also because she was the centre piece of the group. Charlotte wore an orange blouse and dream-catcher ear-rings and her charisma came across loud and clear. It was much more difficult to pick out Connell. Kal spotted him at the edge of the group, looking awkward and lacking the confidence he'd gained with age.

'This is Charlotte,' said Connell. 'I'm sure you must have seen photographs of your mother before now, haven't you Sophie?'

Connell passed the pictures around and Sophie stared at each one. The way Sophie drank in the details made Kal think Raymond hadn't bothered to show her any at all. She felt a new surge of anger – he'd completely neglected his own sister, just when she needed him, throwing her on the rubbish heap and leaving her in the care of others. Whilst he built his own career and his own success. The next time Kal saw him he'd better watch out.

By the time Connell passed around half the photographs the girl's hands were shaking.

'Oh dear, Sophie, are you feeling all right?' asked Connell. 'Perhaps we shouldn't carry on with this today.'

'It's okay,' Sophie said in a small voice. 'I'm fine.'

'Are you sure? There's no rush, my dear,' Connell said.

Kal reacted quickly. 'May I get Sophie a glass of water?'

Connell started to stand up.

'It's no bother, Mr Connell, you carry on here with Sophie. I know where the kitchen is.'

Kal didn't wait for him to protest nor give his agreement and she knew she had a good chance he'd stay to supervise the photographs. She left the room and when Connell didn't follow she ran lightly to the kitchen and filled a glass at the sink. She left the water running. It wouldn't take her long and it was worth the risk.

Earlier, she'd seen a second canvas was placed behind the rider of the apocalypse. Kal eased open the door of the conservatory. Its grating noise was masked by the running water. In a few steps Kal was at the easel and she tilted forward the front canvas.

The image behind took her breath. It was a young woman, naked and kneeling, reclining backwards. The girl's breasts and stomach bore red, angry cuts. Kal heard a noise behind and she turned to find Connell at the door of the kitchen. His body was rigid with fury. If looks could kill, she thought, as she smiled and prepared her excuses.

Connell didn't buy Kal's explanation she'd simply been curious. Afterwards, the interaction between them turned staccato and it wasn't long before they were shown the door.

Without Sophie, Kal knew she'd have been thrown straight onto the street. The only thing she regretted was not having time to take a snap of the image, because she wanted to check with Sophie to see if the girl in the painting was modelled on any of the patients at Melrose. Kal hoped not and she thought it very likely. As soon as possible, Marty must use her internet skills to tap into Connell's employment history and see if it correlated with the string of deaths.

Back in the car, Kal told them what she'd seen.

'Bloody hell,' Marty said.

Sophie looked shocked and didn't say one word and Kal knew Marty would tell her off later for explaining the details so bluntly. Except Kal wasn't the type to withhold information. In her book, Sophie had a right to know.

The rest of the drive passed in silence and Kal began to wonder why Sophie was so quiet. A twinge of conscience told her Marty might be right. Perhaps it had been too much too soon – the photographs, the explicit painting, memories of Charlotte. She couldn't help feeling Sophie had been stirred up again and she didn't have to wait long to find out the consequence. Halfway back to the apartment, Sophie spoke. Her voice had an odd, detached sound.

'I'd like to go back to my parents' house; Lilac Mansions. Please will you take me?'

***

Marty pulled in at a petrol station. The car didn't need filling up but she didn't care. She'd been against taking Sophie to Connell's house in the first place. And what the hell was Kal thinking giving all the lurid details on his sick painting? This was all wrong. Kal wasn't reacting in the right way around Sophie. Not at all.

Marty dribbled two pounds' worth into the tank. Kal got the message because when Marty headed into the shop to pay, Kal trailed after her. Marty rounded on her as soon as they were inside.

'What the hell are you playing at?'

'Wo- ah, calm down.'

'No. I won't. You're gonna push that poor girl over the edge. What is it between you and her? You won't believe she's a suspect. You keep protecting her. Why?'

Marty was slightly taller than Kal. They stood practically nose to nose. Marty knew Kal wasn't the type to be intimidated and she also knew Kal often needed sense pounded into her.

'Why lay all those horrible details on Sophie? And why the hell are we chasing off to this place? She's not ready. You're pushing too hard.'

'I'm not pushing. She wants to go there.'

'Does she? Or is she asking because you already talked to her about it?'

'I never mentioned her parents' place.'

'What is it about Sophie that's got to you? Why are you taking this so personally?'

Kal pressed her lips together. By the time the dust settled in India, Marty had been in a coma. She'd not had time to tell the whole, horrible truth about David Khan. Which was why the secret was festering inside her. When she could stand the humiliation, she'd do it. But not right now.

'Oh, let me think – was it because I found Penny hacked to death on a bed? Oh no, maybe it's because a teenage girl is lying in the morgue and someone's trying to frame Sophie for it.'

'Don't get smart with me, Kal. You know that's not what I mean.'

'Isn't it? Then what are you getting at?'

'You're not thinking straight. You're all over the place and it's not like you. Anyone would think you owe her or something.'

'Bullshit. I'm helping Sophie because she needs help.'

Marty knew Kal wouldn't give in on a head-to-head. There was no point in going further. She'd better try another tactic.

'Think about it. Sophie idolises you. She wants to impress you. Getting stronger is going to take time. It's too soon.'

'Don't be ridiculous, she doesn't ido-'

Marty saw the point hitting home and decided to drive in another nail. Her friend could be bloody-minded and it took a lot of force to turn her off track.

'Talk her out of it,' Marty said, taking her voice down a few notches. 'Let her take one step at a time. You're the right person to help her do that.'

'I know what you're saying, Marty, but Sophie's the link to the murders. I know you think I'm wrong but I'm not. Going to the house might open up memories she's shut away.'

'That's what I'm worried about. She's going to get flooded. What if she needs specialist help afterwards? What're we going to do, take her back to bloody Melrose?'

'No, if necessary we'll take her to a competent doctor.'

'What, you're prepared to go through with it knowing Sophie might not be able to cope? That's damn irresponsible.' Marty shook her head. 'I can't let you do it.'

'Please don't argue.'

Marty swung round and swore under her breath.

'I want to go to Lilac Mansions,' Sophie said. 'Come as my friends, and if not, I'll take a taxi.'

'Listen Sophie,' Marty said, 'I didn't mean…'

'It's okay. I know you're worried about me, it's just,' Sophie shrugged, 'something I've got to do.'

'It's too soon,' Marty said. 'Give it more time. You're barely over the shock of Eliza.'

Marty glanced at Kal, expecting objections, but Kal didn't interrupt because she was scanning her messages. Marty prepared herself for the onslaught – Kal would tell it like she saw it, whether Marty liked it or not.

Putting her phone back in her pocket, Kal placed one arm around Sophie. 'Maybe Marty's right,' she said.

Marty's mouth almost dropped open.

'Maybe rushing isn't such a good idea. Listen, why not leave it until tomorrow and then see how you feel? Sleep on it and we can talk about it in the morning.'

Kal would never back down without a fight. What hell was going on?

'If you think it's best.'

Looking at Kal with those trusting almond eyes, Sophie nodded.

Chapter Thirty-one

To make the rendezvous, Kal left Sophie while she was sleeping. She didn't like tricking Marty nor Sophie but this was something she had to deal with.

On the opposite bank of the Thames, the office blocks didn't have their lights on today, and the tide was much further in than last time. It meant the patch of mud bank where they'd laid Klaus' body was below the waterline.

Kal would have preferred a different meeting place but she had no intention of letting Raphael know. She sat on a low brick wall and waited. Out on the water, a barge made its way up stream, its engine puttering.

'Good afternoon, Kal, I'm so happy you could make it.'

Two men walked towards her. One, short with square shoulders and a muscled torso, squeezed into a dark suit; Clarence the minder, she presumed. The other was younger, around her age. He had dark, shoulder-length wavy hair, a lightly tanned complexion and a model's face with clear cut lines. He walked with a silver-topped cane and a limp which, in her assessment, came from a hip problem, most likely the result of a severe accident.

'Raphael.' She said it as a statement. She must give no hint of weakness right from the word go. And she must make her assessment of him quickly and accurately and give as little away of herself as possible. It was the best way of getting what she wanted out of this interaction.

'The one and only.' Raphael sat beside her, not leaving enough space between them.

He leant towards her, his hair brushing her shoulder. It smelled sweet and clean but Kal wasn't fooled. This man dripped danger. Very likely his temperament was made worse by the fact he'd inherited his power rather than earning it himself. Wealth, power, influence, instability – it was a menacing mix.

Raphael whispered close to her ear. 'Ever taken part in illegal activity, Kal? Is it really your bag?'

'Why shouldn't it be?'

'Seems you were quite the little minx over in India stirring up trouble. Took on more than you could deal with there, didn't you?'

'No.'

'That's why we had to bail you out, wasn't it?'

'Nobody bailed me out.'

Kal kept her tone cold. He'd gone straight in and he was needling around for her weak spot. That's why he'd wanted to meet here, to put her on the back foot. Now he was searching for her vulnerabilities, for what made her twitch. Too bad for him, he'd not be successful.

'Are you really Daddy's girl?' Raphael tilted his head to one side. 'Have you got the balls for it?'

'Listen, I'm here for one thing only and that's to repay my debt. So why the hell don't we stop playing games and get on with it?'

Behind them, Clarence hadn't moved a muscle. Raphael turned to speak to him. 'Goodness Clarence, I'd hoped she was going to be more fun than this, didn't you? She's as boring as hell.'

Clarence didn't comment.

Raphael smiled. A smile without humour and full of malice and she didn't think the malice came from his nasty nature. No, it was a layer worse than that. She felt certain the malice came because Raphael had it in for her. It was personal. And it came from way before this meeting. Raphael already detested her. Maybe that's why he'd requested Kal work for him and her debt to the Cartel be repaid through him? This was more complicated than she thought.

Kal recalled the way Dante rested a protective hand on her shoulder and she was rarely afraid but she knew sometimes it was wise to be. A light sweat prickled her lip. Kal looked towards the grey water of the Thames. She must keep razor sharp. She must get a handle on this. The more she could find out about the source of Raphael's hatred, the better.

'I'm grateful to your father for helping me,' she said, going for the underling approach.

'Yes, I'm sure you are, but then my father wouldn't refuse, would he?'

Why wouldn't the Baron turn her down? Because her father had been one of the Baron's favourites? Because David Khan died avenging the death of the

Baron's older son? And why did Raphael resent that so much?

Raphael pushed on his cane to stand up. 'You even look like him.' The words were full of venom.

'You're talking about my father aren't you? So, you knew him?'

'Who do you think did this to me?' Raphael tapped his cane against his own leg.

Kal didn't answer.

'Everybody knew David Khan, didn't they Clarence?' Raphael spat it out. 'He was a legend in his own lunchtime, haha.'

Jealousy. Envy. Rivalry. Hatred. It was all in there. What had happened between her father and Raphael? Maybe David Khan had crossed Raphael in the past. Maybe he was responsible for the injury? And didn't Dante tell her Raphael had been second favourite? What if his older brother had allied with her father. Whatever the story, Raphael had a nature that fed the resentment, fed it and kept it rolling, and that whole package, that whole, fat agenda had just passed to her. Yes, it made this assignment highly risky. Kal kept her breathing even, knowing Raphael would be scrutinising her for any tiny sign of fear.

'What's the matter? Having second thoughts?' This time Raphael didn't make much effort to hide the goading.

'You can back out if you like, Kal. We won't hold it against you.'

Like hell I will, ass-hole. 'Why would I want to do that?'

187

'Because you must do what *I* say and *exactly* what I say. And this won't be for a novice.'

'Doesn't sound like a problem to me. Let's get it over with.'

'Not so fast, not so fast. We've a timetable to follow and you'll be joining the team. Meet us tomorrow night. I'll send you the address.'

'Right.'

'We've already covered *obedience*, haven't we? Or dog-control as I like to call it. I snap my fingers and you jump, savvy? And there's one other thing I demand from my inferiors and that's punctuality. So don't be late.' Raphael waggled his finger in her face.

He must never see how he got to her. That would be a big mistake. So Kal looked Raphael straight in the eye and gave as meek a nod as she could manage. Raphael's agenda was a nasty complication and it meant the odds were heavily stacked against her achieving her aim of damaging the Cartel.

Up close, she could see tiny broken veins around his nostrils – the mark of an addict.

'That's my girl,' he said with a snigger.

Chapter Thirty-two

Tracking my victims is part of the game – their habits, their favourite take away outlets, what time they take the bus home and which seat they prefer, what movie house they like. I build a detailed dossier. It's part of my ritual and it takes me months. Only once I feel satisfied I know their life inside out, do I plan my move.

That's how I discovered Charlie was a prostitute. She was a popular student by day with a gaggle of hangers-on, and at night she changed into a call girl who strutted her stuff for well-off clients.

I have to be honest and tell you this came as a shock. I'd been seeing her behind the back of her lover for weeks and I had no idea about her clandestine habits. Did it change my view of her? Perhaps it did. Perhaps it made Charlie even more fascinating. For her part, she acted as if she loved her rich boyfriend, whilst seeing me on the side, and trotting out at the weekend with her clients to bring in the cash. So I carried on as if I didn't know her game. Well, why not?

In fact, building my detailed dossier on Charlie became my fascination. My obsession. That's not to say the urge to kill went away because it didn't. What I did to sate it was select other victims whilst I let Charlie live. And since Charlie was a sex worker she naturally turned my interest towards prostitutes. In fact, over the years there were several I used to sate my need to kill.

Even the night in the church left its mark. Charlie was my angel, my saviour, and I fashioned my victims with the halo I'd stared at in the stained-glass windows. As a homage to Charlie.

Now we all know no good comes from lies and deceit, don't we? No surprise then that Charlie could not live forever. She was to come to a nasty end, and all her lovers would play their part in it, though not, perhaps, as we each would have imagined.

Chapter Thirty-three

Situated in London's green commuter belt, the Kendrick family home sat in an exclusive Surrey neighbourhood. Private drives were crammed with expensive cars. The place was awash with alarms and security cameras. Marty parked and turned to face Sophie.

'You're sure you want to go through with this?'

Sophie bit her lip and nodded.

'Okay,' Marty said.

They'd already spent a good hour discussing it over breakfast, and Marty admitted Sophie seemed adamant. She'd also noticed how Kal tried to keep quiet during their talk, presumably to dampen down Sophie's need to impress her. For that, Marty admired her friend. Taking the back seat didn't come easily to Kal.

They walked through the lovely front garden.

'Because no one lived here, I thought the place would be neglected, but the garden is beautiful. Look at it – banks of lavender, roses and those gorgeous delphiniums along the wall, and the lilacs are stunning. The scent of the flowers is over-powering. It's like one of those gardens you pay to go to see,' Marty said.

'My brother hires an agency to maintain it and we've a full-time gardener who cares for the grounds.

Actually, it's the same gardener my mother first hired. It's funny Mr Connell talked about Mum having admirers because I wouldn't have thought about it but I'm sure the gardener was one of them. I remember the way he used to gaze at Mum.'

Sophie paused at the front door.

'You're still sure? Kal asked.

'With you here I feel I can do it. It's a while since I've been back. Last time I fainted and Raymond took me away.'

'You'd better tell us if it gets too much,' Marty said.

Marty watched as Sophie turned the key in the lock. Sophie stepped inside, tripping over the door sill and Marty threw Kal a look of concern as they followed behind.

***

Sophie disabled the alarm and stopped in the hallway. Her mother's flower mural took her breath away - the lilacs and the blues created a masterpiece that must have overwhelmed every guest who came through the door. She remembered how delighted her mother had been, every time someone paused, awestruck. Her mother liked to be admired. Liked to be worshipped. Sophie could see the effect the painting had on Kal and she so wished Kal could be impressed like that by her paintings.

Marty was full of praise too, saying it felt as if Charlotte's painting brought the garden inside the house.

Her mind felt numb and her steps were robotic as she led them to the lounge. What had she expected to find? A bloodstained carpet? Crimson streaks on the floor where her mother had tried to crawl away? Of course not. It was all perfect, with new furnishings and tasteful decoration. Raymond had seen to that years ago.

Kal and Marty trailed behind, treading quietly and careful not to ask questions. She was the guide and they were the followers. She trailed her hand over the golden upholstery of the new lounge furniture. It was lovely, but it had no life in it. And it was not at all what her mother would have chosen.

Sophie looked down the length of the garden. At the far end, down by the willows, Thomas the gardener was stooped over a wheelbarrow. He still had his red hair, recognisable even at this distance, and he appeared, of course, much older than before. She waved and Thomas didn't look up, though he must have known they were there.

'Perhaps we can go and speak to him when we're finished,' Kal said.

Sophie gave a vague nod and headed out into the hallway and up her father's staircase. Mum always said it reminded her of a Hollywood staircase because it was so grand. Sophie put her hand up, pinching her nose to block out the smell of something horrible.

'What is it?' Kal asked.

Sophie shook her head. 'Can't you smell it?'

Kal and Marty exchanged a look. The only thing they could smell was dust.

If Marty hadn't been tired, it might not have happened like it did. Marty was recuperating and stairs seemed to be an issue because she trod heavily as they went up, and then halfway, on Sophie's little landing at the fifteenth step, Marty made to sit down. As Marty sank into the carpet, Sophie felt her world shifting. As if the ground she stood on fell away and she tumbled down a cliff face. Somebody screamed and Sophie screwed her eyes shut.

She felt someone take a firm hold of her arms.

'Keep breathing, Sophie. Look at me, I'm right here, you're safe,' Kal said.

Sophie opened her eyes. She knew she wasn't safe.

A horrible weakness claimed Sophie's legs and they crumpled like spaghetti. It all started to fall apart. A dark mist swirled in and she could hear voices – her father's voice and her mother's voice. The voices of ghosts. My god she was going mad. She couldn't stop screaming and Kal and Marty were carrying her down the stairs. Sophie clutched fistfuls of Kal's hair and hung on. They got her in the car and Marty drove away and Kal sat holding Sophie tight. And she screamed all the way back to 701.

Chapter Thirty-four

Kal sat in the four by four. She kept thinking of Sophie screaming on the staircase with her red mouth open and full of blood where she'd bitten straight through her lip. Push it away, she commanded herself, you can't let it distract you or you're dead.

The back of the car stank of stale sweat and cigarettes. She had three companions, each unknown and dressed as she was in black from head to toe, all the way to their leather gloves. The four of them sat in silence. They stared out at the three other vehicles in Raphael's team. The cars were arranged in a semi-circle in front of a fence topped with razor wire.

She'd arrived on time and they'd now been sitting outside the warehouse for twenty minutes. Where exactly they were Kal couldn't say, since she'd been hooded for the last stretch of the journey. It seemed Raphael wasn't taking any chances with her, and what the warehouse contained and what they were waiting for, she had no idea.

A white van came out of the warehouse and her pulse accelerated. Missing out Kal, Raphael had earlier passed around semi-automatics – guns which behaved like machine guns and were favoured by the low-lives of the underworld. The man next to her stroked his moustache with one hand, his other cradling the metal barrel, fingers light, arm and shoulders relaxed in the attitude of a hardened criminal.

All of the team were hardened. She'd seen it in their attitude, even without hearing their voices. Kal fought the urge to swallow, knowing the sound would reverberate in the silence and mark her out. David Khan had trained her well, but his focus was working as a loner. Keep your nerve, she told herself, you can do it, play it through step by step. Get the goods for Spinks, pay your debt and get out.

The white van pulled up and the limping form of Raphael got out the front seat of one of cars. He tap-tapped his way towards the back of the van. Words were exchanged and then a signal passed. The man next to Kal nodded his head and said one terse word - 'Out'. He had an eastern European accent.

Everyone got out and stood around on the tarmac. Sixteen people in Raphael's team. Eyes front. Focused on the van. Waiting.

Kal didn't look at faces and didn't scan around in an obvious way because she couldn't be sure it wouldn't earn her a bullet in the back. Was Raphael buying or selling, she wondered? What did the van contain? Dante already told her Raphael didn't deal in the Cartel's drug business, so what did that leave? Arms, counterfeit money, chemicals, explosives? What lucrative operations might Raphael have running in and out of London, one of the crime capitals of the world? She itched to get closer.

A limousine cruised along the entrance road to the warehouse. Somewhere on Kal's right, one of Raphael's team coughed. Fingers started to tap on guns. People started to get itchy. This was where it could get tricky. Where a few people might end up dead. Kal knew which way she'd dive for cover. Which way she'd crawl, maybe shielding herself with a wounded or dead body. She hoped to hell it didn't come to that and if it did, that her knee wouldn't let her down.

She couldn't see who got out of the limo, though she was surprised, because from the silhouette it was certainly a woman. And why not? Not all of London's crime scene would be controlled by men.

Raphael accepted a briefcase, presumably containing the pay-off. Then members of the woman's crew got in the van and drove it away, the limo following behind. Was it really so simple? Kal felt the tension draining from her body. If repaying her obligation to the Cartel was as easy as turning up for this handover, this was turning into a disappointment. There was nothing she could do to stop this and very little information she could report back.

She waited for Raphael to dismiss his crew. Except he didn't. It was then her instincts started kicking up.

'It seems we have a little problem,' Raphael said.

No one shuffled. They probably didn't even blink. These people were disciplined.

'Before the handover tonight I double checked the merchandise.'

Raphael was walking amongst them, his cane tapping on the ground.

'I did that last time too and want to know why?'

Tap, tap.

No one replied. All eyes were to the front, military style.

'Because my esteemed colleague, Estelle, has been informing me our shipments fall short of her order.' Raphael's breath misted in the damp night air.

Tap, tap.

'It's so terribly bad for my business. Not to mention, bad for my reputation and bad for my stress levels. You all know how very personally I take anything which affects my stress levels.'

Raphael stopped and no one moved a muscle. Without warning, he whirled, his body moving like a whiplash. The cane came down *crack* on the side of a man's head. The man buckled, his semi-automatic falling with a clatter. No one else moved.

Kal stared. The man on the ground could have reached his weapon. Could have maybe got off a couple of crazy rounds before the others finished him off. *Crack.* Raphael bought his cane down a second time and she saw how his face was contorted with fury.

He pointed in Kal's direction.

'You! Get over here.'

In the dark, she felt the force of his hatred and the relish as Raphael anticipated how he was going to use her. This was going to be bad. Very bad. She had to force herself to walk over. No, she mustn't show any weakness. Not one tiny chink in her façade. She froze her face into a blank mask.

'Get him into the warehouse,' Raphael told her, and she could feel Raphael studying her, hoping to see horror or fear or dismay. Kal showed him none of it and grabbed one arm of the fallen man whilst the man with the moustache grabbed the other.

Inside the warehouse, they strapped him to a chair. The room was stacked with wooden crates and Kal took the chance of glancing in and saw semi-automatics nestling in polystyrene chips. Her skin went clammy. So, Raphael really was one of the big boys. This merchandise would be worth a fortune. Worth maiming for at will.

The man in the chair had a shaven head and a stud ear-ring. Kal wondered how the hell Raphael knew this man was implicated in the missing guns. Or had Raphael simply picked someone at random to force out information? Or to take out his spite on a victim? Make the man an example.

Raphael had the markings of someone unhinged by power and pure evil and he had the backing of the Cartel which made him impossible to oppose. He likely tortured and killed without turning a hair. Kal had a terrible premonition why he'd wanted her involved tonight, and as her own part in it started to warp out of shape, a cold fear took hold of her.

Raphael had regained his composure. 'Go to it,' he told the man with the moustache.

The suspect was stripped to the waist. He then received blow after blow to his face and chest. It was the sound of it which started to get to her – the squelching of meat as his face began to cave. The cracking of his ribs. The man suppressed groans, though no words came out and she wondered how long he'd hold out before he started screaming in agony. Kal felt certain she would throw up and that Raphael would take a delight in it. But it wasn't long before Raphael seemed to grow bored and it confirmed her view – this was every day entertainment for him.

'And what do you make of all this, Kal,' he asked her. 'Is it to your liking?'

He wanted to see her recoil. Wanted to see her horrified.

'This is your business not mine,' she said.

'Oh but I'm making it your business. I think it might be quite fun, don't you, to soften this one up and then you and I can see what you're really made of? A couple of days and he'll soon feel like talking, don't you think?'

'You sick bastard,' she said.

Raphael laughed. 'Ah yes, so now we're starting to get to know each other.'

***

Kal was hooded again and taken from the scene. By then, the victim's face was swollen and blood coursed down his body. He panted, sagging forward against the restraints, but he wasn't yet broken, because his groans had given way to sharp noises of terror before each punch, rather than the screams of a mad man. He would live, she thought, in agony and slowly succumbing to shock or infection because his wounds were not yet life threatening.

They dropped her not far from 701, and Kal held on until the car was out of sight and then threw up in the bushes.

She was trapped in Raphael's sick games. He would try to implicate her, she knew it. Try to write her name on the dead man's body because Kal felt certain it would end in murder. He wanted to punish her for whatever hatred he felt for her father. How the hell was she going to get out of this? How the hell was she going to stop Raphael taking his revenge out on her so she'd owe him for his silence for the rest of her life?

In the toilet of 701, she went into another bout of heaving. Her aim of hurting the Cartel seemed out of reach. They were holding the power and all the cards. So she sat on the bathroom floor and sifted through her father's teachings, searching for her escape route. She must be as clever and as cunning as Raphael, because she knew her life depended on it.

Chapter Thirty-five

Someone was trying to kill her. In Sophie's nightmare, an evil voice pressed into her mind. It drowned out her own thoughts and replaced them with its own vile words.

'Sophie, it's okay, I'm here. You're safe.'

Kal's words came from far away and Sophie could hardly grab on to them. She opened her eyes and tried to tell Kal this was the nightmare she had at Melrose. This was the voice that got inside her head. But the words wouldn't come out. As Kal held her, Sophie listened to herself gibbering like a mad person.

Sometime after, Marty rang the intercom. She'd brought fruit and bagels for breakfast. Sophie took a shower and tried to stop shaking before she joined them.

Marty put a second bagel on her plate and filled it with cream cheese. 'I checked out Connell's employment record and there's no obvious correlation with the deaths of Spinks' women. That doesn't mean much. Connell was in the UK the whole time, so it could have been him. What's our next step? Tracking down Sugar G? Giving Raymond a shake to see what comes out? Kal, are you listening?'

It didn't seem Kal got much sleep last night, she looked washed out. Marty frowned. They needed Kal's full attention, and right now she didn't look capable of giving it.

'Kal? Are you all right?' Marty asked.

'Sure. Melrose is our next step,' Kal said, looking straight at Sophie. 'Your headaches started at Melrose and you keep running away from that place and I want to know why. Then Eliza dies there.'

No kid gloves today, thought Marty. 'An undercover job? You're going to go in below the radar? Are you sure you're up to it? You look pretty rough today.'

'Under the radar, yes, but not me. They know me, which leaves…'

Marty almost choked. 'Shit. You know how I hate anything the wrong side of the law. I can't.'

'It'll be easy. Listen, you've got the perfect, natural cover story so you won't need to make anything up – you were attacked and left for dead, and since then you've not been able to get back on track. It's perfect. You can turn up at Melrose for psychological support. Say you can't face going back to work.'

Marty shifted uncomfortably. 'All of that undercover stuff is your thing. I wouldn't know where to start.'

'Yes, you will. Stay overnight and get as much information as you can. Meanwhile, I'll tackle Sugar G. What do you say?'

'I say "no"', Marty said, knowing full well she had little choice.

***

Marty and Kal headed out and once they'd gone, Sophie threw the rest of the bagels in the bin.

Sitting on the settee, she stroked Purdy. Everyone always commented on Charlotte's artistic abilities. Sophie knew her mother was a show off. As a child, Sophie realised how her mother enjoyed people admiring her. Even perfect strangers. Sophie didn't care, and she didn't care her mother was a prostitute.

A long time ago, Penny told Sophie how her mum got into debt at college. She turned to prostitution and Penny was already in the profession and she'd helped Charlotte cope in those early days. Sophie thought Penny was the best friend her mum ever had.

Sophie guessed Mr Connell hadn't wanted to talk about Charlotte because somehow he knew about the prostitution. And Connell was clever. He'd promised Dr Kaufman he'd not talk about Charlotte, except instead, he talked to Sophie about how her art was so like her mother's – Sophie's choice of colours, the way she viewed and portrayed her work – so similar to Charlotte. He'd brought Charlotte alive in Sophie's imagination. And that's what had started the headaches and the nightmares.

Sophie pressed her fists to her temples. She knew all the memories wanted to come rushing back. Everything she'd packed down threatened to overwhelm her. Like a huge tidal wave come to wipe her out. Did she have the courage? Did she really have the strength to face the truth? To go back to that night and remember it all? She wanted to scream, only this time she didn't. Instead, she crunched up with a cushion and rolled into a ball on the floor.

Kal believed in her. And now it was time for her to believe in herself. Sophie broke out in a cold sweat and her breakfast threatened to return as she allowed the memories to surface.

Chapter Thirty-six

'Good afternoon, Ms King. I see you're scheduled for an assessment with one of our consultant psychiatrists. Let me check, oh yes, you requested Dr Kaufman.'

The receptionist pushed over some papers.

'Please fill these out and take a seat in the lounge. It says you've asked to be admitted for in-patient care and Dr Kaufman will advise you of the possibilities. Please don't worry, you will be thoroughly looked after here.'

At nine hundred pounds per night basic, plus professional fees, Marty was sure she would be.

Marty grabbed the clipboard and the appreciable stack of forms. On top was the medical fee list. This was so not her style. Her hands were sweaty and she felt certain the woman at the desk already knew she was an imposter. Don't be ridiculous, she told herself, you've got as much right as anyone to be here. Just chill out. And Kal was right, Marty wasn't breaking any of her own rules. Gathering information and asking a few questions wasn't criminal behaviour. She could live with it.

Decked out like an exclusive hotel, the lounge had a coffee bar with a mouth-watering range of cakes. The smell of them filled the air. Marty took two and headed for a corner. Classical music played in the background.

Two other people shared the space. A woman in her mid-forties, who was intent on a massive jigsaw puzzle of what, so far, looked like a scene of mount Fuji. The other was a man a little older than Marty, late thirties perhaps. He played a computer car game, earphones plugged to the sides of his head. Marty relaxed a little. This place didn't have the vibe of a psychiatric clinic.

Twenty pages of paperwork and medical questions later, Marty sat back. She ran through the mental checklist Kal had gone through with her – first and foremost she must stick with her story and not veer off it, that was the key to success with any undercover operation, Kal said. Then Marty must chat with any patients she met and find out their take on Melrose. Then get into the adolescent wing and find Seb. And get the lowdown on Kaufman, and then get out. Yes, thought Marty, she was a technical specialist with absolutely no experience of going undercover, but she could do that.

It wasn't long before the receptionist came to find her.

'Ms King, Dr Kaufman is ready for you. This way please, third door on the right.'

***

'In summary, you've been finding it impossible to sleep. The nightmare of being attacked keeps returning in a way which is so real you feel it's happening again. Plus you're experiencing a daytime paranoia of being followed. All this is perfectly normal after a deeply traumatic incident such as the one you describe,' Dr Kaufman said.

Marty agreed, in what she hoped was a convincing way. Forty-five minutes into their consultation and surely Kaufman realised she had no legitimate reason to be here? Kaufman had a clinical, white jacket. Beneath, he wore a blue shirt and tie. Short brown hair, a goatee beard, plain features, no extravagances. She'd place him in his fifties but she couldn't say much more about him – she didn't have Kal's psychological training. Her gut instinct would have to do, and it told her he was an experienced, mature practitioner. A perfectly normal person. Nothing sinister here.

'That's right, doctor,' she said.

'And I see you've described yourself as someone not usually prone to stress.'

'People say I've got my feet on the ground. That's why this is so difficult. It just isn't me.'

'I think our facility will be able to help you through this rough patch, Marty. I recommend daily counselling and afternoon sessions with our relaxation therapist. We'll meet in a week's time to discuss your progress. I'll ask my secretary to prepare the financial details for you, unless, of course, you feel this type of budget is beyond your reach? In which case I could suggest a regime a little more tailored?'

Wow, that was blunt. Patronising bastard. Besides, Sophie was paying for this privilege.

'Your first suggestion sounds perfect,' Marty said. 'It's just the boost I need.'

'Precisely,' said Kaufman.

He signed a form with his gold pen and pushed it across the desk for her signature. Then Kaufman showed her out and he offered his hand. She shook it. How odd, his hand felt smooth like a woman's and she wondered if Kaufman might have some sort of fetish because his skin felt slightly oiled. When she was out of his sight, Marty raised her hands to her nose – they smelled faintly of oranges from whatever products Kaufman used on his skin. Marty smiled, she felt sure Kal would have something deep to say about that.

Marty let out a sigh. Job done. And she mentally ticked the box with Kaufman's name against it.

Marty was good at talking with people. Over coffee and chocolate cakes, she soon found out the woman doing the jigsaw was the mother of twin boys, who'd both joined the army and been killed in action in Afghanistan. The woman was being treated for depression and she carried a picture of her sons in her pocket. Two smiling young men, handsome in their uniforms – no wonder the woman needed support.

The man playing on the console was less forthcoming but once Marty beat his time score on the game, he told her he was a regular at Melrose. He'd been unable to kick his addiction to prescription painkillers which he'd latched onto after a climbing accident in which he fractured his pelvis, his skull and his legs.

Try as she might, Marty uncovered nothing sinister. Everyone she spoke to had nothing but good to report about the clinic, the doctors and the standard of care. This was turning into a waste of time. Why had she been worried about what she was letting herself in for?

Marty's thoughts turned to Kal. How was Kal coping with Sugar G? Shouldn't Marty have gone with her? Damn, don't say she was going to be in the wrong place at the wrong time again.

To make it worse, Marty next had to take part in a private relaxation session in which she spent her time in a flotation tank with dimmed lighting and mood music. All that occupied her mind during the floating was what the hell Kal might be up to, and what risk Kal was putting herself in with no one to watch her back.

It wasn't until later in the evening Marty was able to sneak over to the adolescent wing.

It was a mirror image of the adult side. Marty didn't run into any security and no one stopped her entering.

Kal described Seb as having dark, curly hair and a face which looked like it never smiled. He wasn't in the lounge, nor the dining area, so Marty took her chance down the corridor with the private rooms – a chess player in the lounge had told her which bedroom to look for.

This wasn't criminal activity, but hell, creeping down that corridor Marty felt like a criminal. She felt like she was her low life father. A man who was a mugger and a petty thief. A man who beat Marty's mother. That's why Marty always refused to step over the line and always clung to her own ethics. Because she detested deception. Detested lies. Detested-

'Hey, adult patients aren't supposed to come over this side. You'll get in trouble.'

It was Seb, she was sure of it. He looked so solemn and grim.

'I was looking for you,' she said.

'Wayne told me a black woman was after me,' Seb said, eyeing her suspiciously.

Kal had told her about Eliza's terrible history and she'd recounted Sophie's own story. Now, with this young man in front of her, Marty suddenly knew why Kal stepped over the line. Why she took risks. Yes, she did it because sometimes people were so hurt, like Seb, you couldn't do anything except reach out to help them.

Seb stepped back. 'And Wayne told me to watch out.'

Slowly, Marty put her hand in her pocket and pulled out a piece of rose quartz. The pink crystal fitted in her palm. It had come from Kal's apartment and Sophie said it was just the thing Seb loved.

'I brought something for you, from Sophie.'

'Is this a trick?'

'No, I need to talk to you, it's about Sophie and-'

'Stop right there.'

Marty swung round.

'Ms King what are you doing in the young people's quarters? Step back, Seb, I believe she could be dangerous. Well done young Wayne for raising the alarm.'

Dr Kaufman had his hand on the shoulder of the chess player from the lounge, presumably Wayne. As the doctor's other hand came into view, Marty recoiled. Kaufman held a syringe.

'What the hell do you think you're doing? Get away from me with that shit.'

But Kaufman was on her in a second. He pushed the needle into her skin.

'Stay calm, Marty. You've placed yourself in my care and I intend to fulfil my obligations.'

Marty's legs turned to jelly and she sat down with a thud. 'This is wrong, I'm not ill. I want to leave.'

'I'm sorry, Marty,' said Dr Kaufman, 'my assessment has shown otherwise, and you've given me full authority to treat you. You will be well cared for at Melrose, don't you worry.'

No, no, she thought, scrabbling to stay upright. Her vision was blurring with Kaufman going in and out of focus and Marty toppled, face first onto the carpet.

Chapter Thirty-seven

At every vibration of her phone, Kal jumped, dreading it to be her summons back to the warehouse. Raphael had her trapped. He had her sweating just like he wanted. She could hardly think straight and that spelled danger. *Don't let the enemy mess with your mind. Never let the enemy infiltrate your thoughts.* If you did, they'd won.

She chose black jeans and t-shirt. She must be stealthy and not raise any suspicions. So she added lip colour and left her hair loose. It was time to confront Sugar G.

Montgomery Road lay quiet and she entered the alley behind. The houses had back-to-back gardens and it was impossible to know if she was being watched from the neighbouring properties. Too bad – she'd take the risk.

Kal leapt a fence and then another, and went through the gardens until she reached the back of number forty-one. Running for the cleaning closet window, she found it closed and the tools she'd brought didn't budge it. Damn.

She searched the back of the property. The windows were sash style and there would always be an opening – a loose latch, a round bathroom ventilator which could be knocked through, an unlocked or faulty basement door. Kal looked carefully until she found where human nature had won against all the security warnings; one of the kitchen windows was cracked open for ventilation. Perfect.

Inside, she focused on sounds. A dripping tap. The hum of an appliance. She waited, crouched by the kitchen sink. No voices. No footsteps. No television or radio. The room smelled of toast. In front of her, the counter was strewn with bread and jars of jam. Kal made her way to the door. Most of the women must be asleep at this time of day, recovering after a long night.

In case someone took her by surprise, Kal grabbed a piece of toast, ready to take a huge bite and mumble a 'hello' with her mouth crammed full. It would probably be enough to put most people off the trail. Her adrenalin was pumping as she headed down the corridor.

'C-l-i-c-k'

She'd never forget the sound of her father's gun at her temple. Nor the sweat and fear which slicked her back when she became confused.

In the pitch black of the bunker, David Khan had set her a task. Find him. Or he would find her.

Patches of grit peppered the concrete floor. By that time, she'd learned to be stealthy. She was good at it. Relished the challenge of moving without a trace. So silent. No breath, no current of air to betray her. How to track your target in the dark. How to prevent them finding you. Speed could be your enemy but it could also be your friend. Watch out because your mind could play tricks. Your own fears or your desire to succeed – they could both trip you up. Stability of mind, focus and a trained body – they were the keys.

She had been so close.

'C-l-i-c-k.' Her father's gun was at her temple.

The sound made her heart stop.

'Better than last time,' he said, his voice icy. 'Now let's do it again.'

Keeping her footsteps light, she navigated her way to Sugar G's games room. This was the place she must get answers.

Kal tossed the bread and gave the door a tiny push with her fingertips. It swung quietly open and her heart rate spiked when she saw Sugar G's back. He was in front of a console, with headphones on. This would be tricky. She hoped to get what she wanted without them maiming each other which meant she'd have to play it by ear.

Kal flexed her fingers. Her father had taught her Dim-mak – the ancient art of using pressure points to inflict serious injury. Once he'd fought her half to death with it and told her it was a valuable lesson. As she tiptoed across the room, she had a flash of insight – she didn't need to drown in her father's poison, she was using it to help those in need. She really could turn the bad into the good.

A tension stole into Sugar G's shoulders as his unconscious told him someone was behind him. Kal waited for him to speak. Words would be better than violence.

'Stay right where you are,' Sugar G said.

In the few moments of quiet, she heard her own pulse thundering in her temples.

Sugar G ripped off his headphones and swung to face her.

'How did you know?'

There'd been no cameras and no electronic detection as far as she could tell. But a certain type of person knows when there's an intruder. Especially someone as used to living under the radar as Sugar G.

'You think I'm stupid?'

He flung aside the leads and the metal ends bounced on the table top. 'I knew you weren't looking for damn work.'

Sugar G rested both hands on his thighs and he sounded icily calm. It told her she'd better be very careful. People who kept the anger out of their voice and kept it in their body were those who snapped. A trickle of sweat ran down her back.

'I don't like being played with,' Sugar G said. Menace filled the room like something solid. 'Who the hell are you?'

Should she carry on her cover story? Spin him a yarn about running away after Penny's murder and now being scared? No, there was only one strategy which could take the sting out of Sugar G's desire to slice her.

'I'm nobody, but my father was a highly-skilled infiltrator. So, if you like, I take after him.'

'And what?' he said.

'I'm here to help Sophie.'

He got to his feet and she knew he wanted to draw his knife.

'We don't have to kill each other,' she said. 'We both want the same thing.'

'You don't know what the fuck I want.'

He started circling her and she turned with him and kept her face towards him, her arms loose by her sides, her knees flexed.

'I know Penny looked after Sophie when Charlotte died,' she said. 'I know Penny tried to help her and I know Charlotte was a prostitute. Did you know Charlotte?'

'Aren't you the clever one,' he said, his eyelid drooping more as his anger mounted. The veins on his arms were standing out and it told her he was ready to spring. When he did, a low dive or a somersault, aikido style, would take her under the arc of his arm and bring them to the floor. Then she must get a Dim-mak lock on him. If she could. Sugar G would have the physical advantage and the force of passion.

'We can talk about this,' she said. 'I know you're not the killer.'

That wasn't strictly true. It was a matter of degrees. Sugar G could be the killer but was he *enough* of a loner? Was he twisted *enough*? And if he and Penny were lovers, what would be his motivation? She needed more.

'Liar. I'm the number one suspect. The police are wetting themselves to charge me.'

His hand went behind his back and the blade glinted as he pointed it towards her face.

'I don't have much to lose if I gut you.'

Kal tilted her chin. 'If you're going to kill me then tell me the truth. You were the first person in the room after Penny died, weren't you?'

He slowly shook his head.

Of course, no, Sophie had been the first in the room and him the second. Then he'd taken her downstairs and come back up. And by that time, Kal had arrived. And she'd guessed right, the gold paint had been left on Penny by Sophie.

'You took Sophie away.'

Sugar G didn't answer but he slowed his prowling.

'Who else was messing in the Kendricks' lives around the time they were killed? Who had a motive?'

Also, if Sugar G wasn't Penny's killer and he knew who was, wouldn't he have murdered them by now? For taking away Penny.

'Why the hell should I help you.' He spat on the floor.

'Because I'm the only one who can help Sophie.'

Something was getting through to him. She could see him turning over the options. Sugar G shook his head again.

'Like I said earlier, who the hell are you? You're not the law, I can see that.'

Kal said nothing.

'If you must know, Charlie was married to a stinking-rich doctor. He doted on her, but she was a high-class call girl when they married and he didn't even know it. There were one or two clients she kept contact with. She'd see them occasionally for fun. Penny said being the wife of a wealthy man was boring as hell. I guess he didn't have what it takes.'

'Right.'

He ran his finger across the flat of his knife, light glanced off steel as he twisted the hilt.

'You're a strange one and you've got balls walking in here.'

'Tell me about it.'

Right at that moment, he sprang at her and she jumped him. They both slammed into the floor and her reflex for survival took over. Sugar G was quick but Kal had a one-hand hold on the pressure point at his neck when Sugar G started laughing and rolled onto his back.

Kal let go. She rolled to her feet and out of reach. 'What the f-'

'Aren't you a bag of surprises.'

Sugar G was still laughing when he stood up. 'You remind me of someone else. She was a deadly bitch, just like you and I was kinda sorry to see the back of her.'

She kept her eye on him. And her distance. The bastard had jumped her right at a moment when it was natural to let her guard down a little. Right when he'd begun talking. Now she started circling him.

'Penny always figured it was a jilted lover who did them in,' he said. 'Shot Martin from jealousy and then killed Charlie to spite her.'

'Names?'

'No idea.'

He'd parked his butt on the edge of a desk. 'The person who killed Charlie and Penny is out there, walking around scott-free,' he said. 'And you'd better find 'em before I do.'

Sugar G was a sadistic bastard. The type to gut a rival pimp or scar the face of one of his girls if they crossed him. And he was one crazy piece of shit. But she'd got what she wanted, she'd pushed enough to know he didn't fit her serial killer profile.

Sugar G swung the point of the knife towards the door.

Kal got the message. If she didn't leave, they'd have to take it further.

'Sophie's on her own now,' he said. 'And if you find who killed Penny, do me a favour, don't let him live.'

Kal backed off, then she walked out and didn't look back.

Chapter Thirty-eight

I told my first victim I was a student of mathematics. This was a lie. My father was a top consultant at a London medical school and he forced me to follow the same profession. It was pointless to fight against his wishes. Since I'm way above average intelligence, my medical studies were no obstacle and besides, my education helped me in drugging and slicing my targets, so I shouldn't really complain, should I?

When I qualified, I continued in medicine.

And what of my angel?

I kept paying her homage with my victims. And she got married and had a daughter.

When I was forced to kill Charlie I was devastated. But what do you think is almost as good as the original? Well, a replica of course.

Little Sophie proved to be an excellent replica.

And she was the one who would never get away.

Chapter Thirty-nine

Marty stared up at the white ceiling. She felt nauseous. Oh, yes, that's right, she was in hospital, recovering from the alley attack.

Turning her head to look at the children's playground, she found instead a blank wall. The window was located on the opposite side of the room, and looked out at the sky. That was strange. She must've moved rooms. Marty edged herself up the bed and was surprised to find her arm tugging on a plastic tube attached to a drip. That was odd too, perhaps she'd had some kind of relapse because she thought she'd been taken off intravenous. Whatever they were pumping into her was messing with her head because she couldn't think straight and couldn't remember how she'd got here.

Marty slumped back on the pillows. She'd gone home hadn't she? Wasn't all this over? She could remember her brother and LeeMing laughing at her flat. Recalled her mother happy on the drive home. Or was that wishful thinking? Fantasies brought on by her struggle for recovery and by her frustrations and the hard fact that she still had hours to put in on the bloody treadmill?

Later, she jerked awake as the door opened. A nurse came in and changed over the bag on the drip.

'What's happened? Did I have a fall? I thought I'd be discharged soon?'

'You rest, Ms King. Everything is fine.'

'I don't feel fine. I feel… strange.'

'Dr Kaufman has you on sedatives which might have an odd effect – they're designed to calm you down.'

'Dr Kaufman? I'm not sure I know him.'

'Don't you worry, just lie back. You can speak to the doctor in the morning.' The nurse smiled and pattered out.

'Wake up.'

'Go away,' Marty muttered.

'Wake up. It's me, Seb. You've got to wake up, you're in danger.'

'What?'

It was night time now and Marty could make out the shape of a young boy standing by the side of her bed. He seemed a young teenager. She reached to turn on the light and couldn't find the switch.

'Don't. They mustn't know I'm here.'

There was an urgency in the boy's voice.

'Listen, I feel like shit and if this is some kind of joke…' she said.

'Remember this?'

The boy held up an object. He twirled it in front of her eyes and street light filtering in showed a crystal of some kind, or a stone. Thing was, she sort of did recall it, but the memory kept slipping away. He put it in Marty's hand. It was hard and rough.

'You were giving this to me from Sophie. Then Dr Kaufman drugged you. You need to get that thing out of your arm.'

'I don't know who you are or what you want, but you'd better get out of here.'

'I've seen how Kaufman controls people. Kaufman controlled Sophie. Eliza and Sophie used to sleep in the same room a lot, you know, since they were kids. I think Eliza knew something. Maybe Sophie said some stuff in her sleep, I don't know, but I know Sophie had nightmares. And Kaufman got it out of her.'

'Got what out? What are you talking about?'

'He got to know whatever Eliza knew about Sophie and then he killed her.'

'Wait – I think you're confused. This is a reputable London hospital with professional staff and there's no need to be afraid. I'll come with you and we'll go and find a nurse and-'

'Wrong. This is a loony bin full of people like me who've got no one. Kaufman can do what he wants. He's the king around here. You've got to get out and-'

The door swung open and the light blazed on. In walked a man with short brown hair and a goatee beard and a doctor's white jacket.

'What are you doing here, Seb?' he said, in an easy voice. Marty saw he aimed the question not at the boy but at her.

'He just walked in and started talking about his friends. I couldn't follow anything he was saying.'

The doctor was friendly and he held out a hand and Marty noticed how Seb cowered.

'He didn't do any harm, doctor,' she said.

'Of course not,' said the man in the white coat. 'Come on now, Seb, let's get you back to your bed.'

As he led the boy away, the doctor glanced back at Marty and Marty didn't know why but she closed her hand over the crystal, hiding it from view.

The light went off and Marty lay in the dark.

Listening to their footsteps fading, she turned the crystal over and over. It didn't stir any memories. How odd. It disturbed her the boy was scared. And how had he found his way up here from the children's wards? Why had he been wandering around in the middle of the night? She didn't see how that could have happened. Seb, he said his name was, and now Marty regretted not asking for his full name so she could go and check he was okay.

She swung her legs over the edge of the bed and opened the door of her locker to find her phone. It wasn't there and neither were her clothes, nor her get-well-soon cards. She lay back down. It was giving her a headache trying to figure it out. Of course, the boy would be fine, the nurses would look after him. Perhaps the drugs he was on had made him confused? But still, his look of fear didn't sit well with her. And what had happened to her things? Why would she move room and her personal effects not come with her? Probably she was fatigued from all the bloody testing and she couldn't remember the explanation. Yes, that might be it.

Every time she closed her eyes, Seb was imprinted on her eyelids. What if he'd been telling her something important? No, that was ridiculous. Well, it might have been important to him but it was just made up, it was crazy talk. *Come on Marty, you're the one with your feet on the ground, there's no room here for conspiracy theories.* Still, Marty would have liked to speak to Kal. And to get it straight in her head.

After over an hour of not being able to sleep, Marty couldn't stand it any longer. What the hell, she thought, it wasn't like she was at death's door anymore, and a few hours without drugs wouldn't do any harm. She'd do it simply to satisfy the little voice in her head that wouldn't shut up. The one which kept telling her something was wrong. So she reached up and turned off the drip.

Chapter Forty

The second summons came as Kal left Montgomery Road.

This time it was the three of them – Kal, Raphael and Clarence the minder. Kal sank into a dark mood, staring out of the car window, as they left behind the London suburbs and headed into the fields and countryside of Kent. As she'd suspected, this time they didn't head towards the warehouse. But the tracker in her shoe should let Spinks know where they were going. She only hoped one of Spinks' team was vigilant enough to notice she'd left the capital.

'All these lovely unpatrolled waters, miles and miles of it – the Kent coastline is full of estuaries and deserted marshes, literally minutes from London. Perfect for bringing in armaments under the radar, and,' Raphael glanced at Kal, 'other goods.'

My god, he was showing off. *Use all information to your advantage*, said the voice in Kal's head. Yes, she must find Raphael's weaknesses. This man who was the second favourite, what could she sense in him to exploit? What could give her a lever to walk out of this alive? And still take an axe swing at the Cartel, while she had the chance.

Twenty minutes later, Kal spotted a sign for the Medway estuary. Mudflats stretched into the distance. She didn't know this part of Kent but she knew Raphael was correct. Small boats would go undetected here because it wasn't high profile enough to have coastguard patrol. In fact, Kent had done everything to build up the reputation of the estuaries as wildlife and significant wetland reserves, to be protected for nature and biodiversity.

Up ahead, amongst the waterbirds and the reeds, two barges lay low in the water. The rusty hulks had long been abandoned and left to rot.

Cutting the engine, Clarence parked close by. Then they walked a narrow track down to the water and found a concealed dinghy. It was a remote spot, not suitable for most vehicles and with no public access, so not many dog walkers and joggers would come this way. A couple of bursts from the dinghy engine and they were soon alongside the second of the barges. They climbed aboard and Clarence unlocked the hatch.

Raphael's victim was in the small space of the main cabin. The worst thing was the smell – stale urine and blood, sweat and fear. The man had been there almost eighteen hours but it looked like days – his skin was ashen, his face swollen to grotesque proportions, and his chest had caved on one side and was black. Kal made certain to conceal her horror.

'My, what a mess,' she said, peering into his eyes. One was puffed closed and he wasn't able to focus with the other. He'd lost plenty of blood and been left without water. In the grip of dehydration, blood loss and shock, only his good physical condition was keeping him from a cardiac arrest. If he didn't get medical help soon, he was finished.

'So Kal, what do you think we should do with him? He's already confessed his guilt and he's no use to me now, except, of course, as an example. Perhaps I should thank him for giving my team a reminder of my temper?'

She shrugged.

'Don't act all high and mighty. Your father would have done the same. He always believed in making a show of people who stepped out of line,' Raphael said.

Her blood ran cold. Raphael would get off by taunting her about David Khan's brutality, and what resistance did she have? Her father was her weak point. If Raphael realised, she would stand no chance.

The man in the chair gave a sickly gulp and she eyed him dispassionately.

'I hoped you'd be able to tell me more about my father,' she said to Raphael. 'He was my mentor. I wish I'd had chance to work alongside him like you did.'

'Yes, I suppose,' Raphael said. 'That's why I thought we should have a little test. A little trial of your abilities.'

Kal raised an eyebrow. 'What a good idea. I like challenges.' And she smiled.

Raphael held out his hand and Clarence passed over a revolver which wasn't a modern model. It reminded her of a collector's piece. She imagined Raphael kept it for this type of occasion. Perhaps he had his favourite torture instruments for any number of circumstances. She noticed too, how Raphael pulled on a pair of leather gloves, and there were none for her.

Raphael checked the barrel, tipped out all but one bullet and spun the barrel shut with a click. So, they were to play a game of Russian roulette. Like in some old, Western movie.

'One bullet in the chamber,' Raphael said. 'I saw David Khan play this game several times.'

'Who with?'

'Now, now, Kal, I'm the one asking the questions, remember? I'm the one in charge.'

Raphael placed his cane to the side.

'Who are your accomplices?' Raphael asked the man. His tone was almost conversational.

The man gave no reply.

'Ladies first,' Raphael said with a smirk.

She could see how he was enjoying this – Raphael was almost pissing himself.

Kal weighed the gun in her hand. 'This is an antique. If you'd have told me, I could have brought my own weapon.' And then, she thought, she'd have more chance of guessing if it would be a blank. When you know your own as well as she did, the weighting of it in your hand could suggest if a lone bullet was in the chamber. Kal took aim. She would have to make it a miss, but convincing enough.

Bam.

Kal fired at the man's shoulder. It was a blank and she felt the wave of relief. She handed the gun to Raphael and he gave her a shrewd look.

'Shoot to kill or you'll be the one with the bullet in your head,' he said softly. Kal flicked her hair back and put her hand on her hip.

Raphael raised the gun, aiming at the man's head. *Bam.*

Another blank. Kal realised she'd been holding her breath and she mustn't do that because Raphael would notice. He might notice too how her legs had started to shake. No, she must play for time and take the risk right now of goading Raphael.

'My father wasn't as much of a sick bastard as you,' she said.

'Yes, he was. You saw him through rose-tinted glasses.'

'Is that how you see your own father?'

She felt fury run through him, and was it her imagination or had Clarence twitched? Good.

'My father… my father…' Raphael wagged his finger in her face and she knew finger wagging was one of Raphael's giveaways. Good again.

Your father what? Come on, spit it out. I'm running out of time.

'… believes in me.'

Bingo. Raphael wanted his father's approval and he didn't have it. He wanted his father to believe in him and see him as a success.

Raphael handed the gun back to her and she looked down at it and ran her finger along the barrel.

'You and I could make a great team, don't you think?' she said slowly. 'My father taught me *everything* he knew. Wouldn't that be an asset to your operation?'

'Let's finish off the business at hand. I really don't think you've got anything I want.'

'You might be surprised. My father's techniques are known only to me. Perhaps I might be the one to give you the edge against your competitors, to push you to the very top of the pyramid. King of the underworld. It would be impressive, wouldn't it?'

Raphael licked his lips. She'd got his attention.

'Shoot to kill, and we can talk later,' he said. 'You're one of us. And the Cartel is the only place where you won't feel judged. Where your skills will be valued.'

Wrong.

Clarence brought his gun to aim at Kal's head. She couldn't stall any longer and this time, she couldn't fake it. The gun felt as if it weighed two tonnes as she sighted on the man's chest. Only two blank chances left out of three, and those were odds she didn't want to take.

Kal controlled the shake in her arm as sweat trickled down her temple. Come on, Spinks, where the hell are you? Her finger curled against the tension in the trigger. She strained for any warning shouts outside, or the sound of a motor boat. The man's chest was moving in time to his rapid breathing and she focused on his right nipple. She could feel Raphael's excitement and his scrutiny of her. She would squeeze in the space between two of her own breaths. Could she gauge it to perfection and miss the man's vital organs yet still pierce his chest cavity? She thought she could do it. But what if she got it wrong? The slightest error and the man would die. How would she live with that? But if she didn't take the risk she would die herself, she was sure of it – Clarence would shoot her. A chest shot was her only chance. Or should she spin at the last minute and take out Raphael? Surely he would have anticipated it? Or was he too arrogant to consider it? Then, as Kal prepared to fire, she heard the screech of tyres at the bank. About bloody time.

'Police,' Clarence said, dead pan. Pulling around his semi-automatic, he made for the hatch, firing as soon as he exited.

'Fuckers!' screamed Raphael. He didn't hesitate and followed behind Clarence, his own weapon firing in bursts.

When Spinks and his team poured through the hatch, Kal stood slowly with her hands in the air and Spinks read her her rights and arrested her, so her cover stayed intact. The man in the chair and anyone else would never be alerted to the fact she was an informant.

Chapter Forty-one

Sophie pressed her fists to her temples, grinding her knuckles in until it hurt. She knew soon the nightmare images would crowd her into a corner. Hadn't she known this would happen if she went back to Lilac Mansions without the protection of medication? Yes, she'd suspected.

Pain flashed deep inside Sophie's head. This time, it would overwhelm her. The pain would be unbearable. This time she wouldn't have any drugs to dull it down, leaving her in a stupor. This time she'd face it. Sophie dug her nails into her palms and screwed her eyes shut.

With her back to the wall, she slid to the floor and then crawled to the corner and her safe barricade behind the settee. Except it wasn't safe, was it? Nowhere was. And she wasn't ready. She'd never be ready. But hadn't Kal shown her she could do it? That she was strong enough? That when it came, she would be able to withstand it? Sophie pressed her fists harder into her head. Do it, she told herself, just do it.

She curled into a ball and she was so frightened she cried. Part of her had always known she'd need to be alone when this moment came. Sophie bit down on her knuckles. Do it. Go back to the house, she told herself.

Go back and walk down to the fifteenth step. In her mind's eye, Sophie counted off each stair – one, two, three… eleven, twelve. She shook so hard, her head banged against the floor. Thirteen, fourteen. And, in her mind's eye, on the fifteenth step, Sophie sat down and she let herself remember.

It was a big house and Sophie was quiet on her feet. This wasn't the first time she'd sneaked to listen to adult conversations when she shouldn't. And it gave her a thrill when she got away with it, so the thrill had become as much a temptation as the listening itself.

She sniffed the sprig of rosemary and tossed it back on her pillow, then swung her legs quietly to the floor. This wasn't an ordinary conversation between her mother and father. It was an argument. Which made it even more daring, since her parents rarely raised their voices. It spiked Sophie's curiosity.

Her father's staircase was lushly carpeted in red. Sophie loved its elegant curve and polished balustrade and she had her very own special place half way down – a little landing, fifteen steps from the bottom and fifteen steps from the top, right where the staircase curved. In bare feet, she crept along the top landing and started to go down.

Her father was getting angrier and it sent a shiver up her back. She could hear her mother too, speaking quietly and in a strange way. It was only once she'd made it to her special spot Sophie was able to put a name to the tone in her mother's voice – pleading – and that's when she started to wish she'd stayed in bed.

Sitting down, she rested her head against the balustrade. She felt glued to the carpet and she shivered, though not from the temperature because it was a warm evening. No, it was the violence she could hear which made her tremble. And then – *Bang*. It was the loudest noise she'd ever heard and she jumped so hard she hit her head on the balustrade. Everything went quiet.

After a while, her mother's pleading started again and then this too stopped, and Sophie heard instead her mother's bloodcurdling screams. The little girl clutched the balustrade. She screwed herself as small as possible. She squeezed shut her eyes. But she couldn't block out the horrible sounds.

How much later she opened her eyes, she couldn't say, and she really wished she'd kept them shut. A man stood at the bottom of the stairs. He was dressed in black, with a horrible, dark balaclava pulled over his face. All she could see was his eyes. Sophie wished hard that she'd disappear except it didn't happen. She wished the man would disappear and that didn't happen either. He was heading up the stairs.

She began whimpering, staring at the man's black shoes, one of which had two spots of blood on its shiny surface. Sophie's heart almost burst with terror when he reached out his gloved hand and placed his fingers under her chin. He tilted her head up. She dare not look at his eyes. Instead, she stared at the skin between his glove and sleeve, inches from her nose so that her quick breaths seemed to bounce off his white wrist, and she could smell his skin and from it came the distinct fragrance of oranges. Blind terror and death and blood mingled together in her head. She knew her parents were dead. And this man would kill her.

Something snapped and Sophie died. Not in the same way as her parents. In a different way, so that part of her sanity was lost, and she ran away to hide in a small space in her mind where she would forever lock away the terror. And with it, she locked away her memories.

By the time the man let go her chin and walked away, part of Sophie had gone. Gone away to protect her, and the Sophie that was left could remember nothing.

Sophie awoke alongside a pool of her own vomit. Now she understood – the shouting from downstairs, her descent, the noises of death and murder, her mother's screams, and the man who'd killed them.

And she remembered that terrible smell – the smell of oranges.

It was Kaufman. How she hated him.

Sophie closed her eyes and she cried for the loss of her parents and, for the first time, cried for herself as the little girl who'd been left alone. Yes, she had gone over the edge that night. That's why she smashed things and didn't know why. That's why she stabbed people and couldn't remember anything about it afterwards – she'd stabbed a school teacher, more than one of the nurses at Melrose, Eliza, Kal. And she knew she'd done those terrible things to make sense of the trapped feelings and to try to get them out – feelings which could never be understood without the memory of that night.

Murderous feelings that welled up from her core, that came from anguish and pain and torment.

Sophie sat up. A long time passed before she went to the bathroom where she splashed her face with cold water and stared at herself in the mirror. Her legs no longer trembled and her almond eyes looked steadily back at her.

Now Sophie understood why the headaches started at Melrose earlier this year – it was because her memories were trying to push through. Perhaps that's what they'd been trying to do all along, and the drugs had stopped it and then Mr Connell's arrival had tipped the balance.

Yes, it was all clear to her now – how her doctor had manipulated her. The murdering bastard. Sophie felt a hot, unfamiliar sensation in her chest and she knew what it was – rage. A rage that had been dormant underneath layers of fear and panic and confusion. That must be why she felt so different. She was a new person ready to take action. Only one word came to mind – revenge.

Chapter Forty-two

'Good morning, Marty. Are you feeling better today?'

'Thank you doctor, much better.'

'Oh,' said Kaufman, 'what happened to your drip?'

'I pulled it over going to the bathroom. The nurse said not to worry since it was finished and I'd be getting a new one later.'

Kaufman nodded and Marty kept what she hoped was a fazed-out expression, and not one which was too stupid. Of course, some people still assumed any black person was an idiot or mentally deficient, and if her luck was in, Kaufman might be one of them. Good, because she needed all the help she could get to cover over her poor acting skills. Marty closed her eyes.

'I've decided to move you to another facility.'

She stared blankly at his white coat.

'Am I ready to go back to my apartment? That's a relief.'

'Not your apartment yet, no, but I think the new facility will be more suited to your needs,' Kaufman said smoothly.

My god, thought Marty, if she hadn't already worked out she wasn't at St George's Hospital where she'd been operated on after the assault, she'd have been taken in by this man's calm authority.

After Seb's visit, she'd found the Melrose Clinic brochures out at reception. Stumbled around on numb legs and found too, a woman who'd been picking at the pieces of a jigsaw puzzle at two o'clock in the morning. The woman filled Marty in about where she was, and, most probably, why.

Well, Marty knew she wasn't mentally ill, but she couldn't yet recall exactly why she was here. Except she knew it was something important and something to do with Kal, and she felt certain her reason for being here was connected to the boy, Seb, who'd come to see her last night. That was the only reason she'd gone back to bed – because Seb's room had been empty and Marty had no intention of leaving until she found him.

'A new facility? Oh, all right then, if you say so,' Marty said with a smile.

'Come on then,' Kaufman said, holding out his hand.

He didn't believe in wasting time, did he? Marty threw back the sheet, ignoring the fact she was dressed in a flimsy hospital gown. She pushed on a pair of slippers, her feet clumsy, still lacking sensation. Obviously, when people were full of whatever drug he'd had her on, they were compliant and passive, so she'd better not offer any resistance. Marty stood up, swaying slightly so she had to hold onto the bed for support.

Kaufman offered his arm and within a few minutes they'd negotiated a corridor and a fire exit without seeing a single person. Marty's legs felt twice their usual weight and her arms didn't react immediately, as if there was a time delay between her thoughts and muscle action.

As Marty trod across the tarmac towards what she assumed was Kaufman's car, she thought through her options. Should she simply knock him out and call the police? She felt certain she could do it, in spite of the physical effects of the drugs. What evidence did she have of wrong-doing if she took that course? Would it help her find Seb? Kaufman would have it all tied up, wouldn't he? He'd make her sound like a hysterical head-case and the boy was in trouble, that was for sure. Marty shook her head to try to clear more of the fog and to speed up her thoughts, which still crawled at half speed. Think, woman, think, she told herself.

As she neared the car, Marty's questions were answered when she saw a dark, curly head resting against the window. Seb was already in Kaufman's car. Excellent. Now she could take the doctor out with one blow and that would be a pleasure.

With a click, Kaufman turned off the central locking. Marty positioned herself ready to strike, and it was then she saw the drool running down Seb's chin and the strange way Seb stared into space. She hoped the shock didn't show on her face.

Kaufman put his hand on her shoulder and too late, Marty realised he'd given her another injection. Damn, she wasn't as vigilant as she thought – there must still be much more drug in her system than she realised.

'Very clever,' Kaufman said. 'But not clever enough. Get in.'

And Marty's knees were already caving as she folded herself in beside Seb.

Chapter Forty-three

Sophie had waited long enough for Kal. What could possibly have happened for Kal not to have come home? She'd promised to return, but Sophie couldn't sit here and wait and do nothing, like she'd always done. Not now she knew the identity of her parents' killer. She knew the identity of the man who'd murdered Penny and dear Eliza. Kaufman, she thought, how she loathed him.

Doctor Kaufman with his fetish for orange-scented hand cream. Yes, she must have buried the connection all these years, but at Melrose, Kaufman's hands were always so smooth, so feminine, and they always had a faint scent of orange from the expensive cream he used. That night on the stairs, she'd smelt the same scent. Now she knew it had been him.

Thoughts swirled in her head. She'd been duped for years. Pulled along like a lamb on a string, dancing to Kaufman's tune, punched into a stupor by his medication, made to believe she was weak and fragile and would never cope. When all the time Kaufman made sure she always stayed within his clutches where he could control her. No more, she vowed. Never, never again. Time to stand up for herself. Time to strike back.

Strike back for her parents and for her friends. She wasn't a defenceless little girl anymore, this was a new Sophie. And Kaufman was an evil, murdering monster.

***

A bunch of women were already working Montgomery Road. Nobody paid Sophie much attention and the woman who opened the door only put up a little resistance.

'For God's sake Soph, don't let Sugar G find you here or he'll go ballistic. You've got to stay clear of this place.'

'I only want to grab a few things, you know, my make-up stuff. I promise I'll be gone in a couple of minutes.'

'Okay but don't tell anyone I let you in, promise?'

In the hallway, the woman gave Sophie a hug.

'Be quick, hun,' she said, and Sophie nodded.

Up in the rainforest room, Sophie swept her supplies into a bag and then slid open the closet. Inside was a clutch purse Penny had given her, containing a knife and a pepper spray. "Every girl should have one," Penny had said with a smile, "you never know when you might need it."

She stuffed a matching dress studded with sequins into her bag. Penny had given them to her for her last birthday, and Sophie already decided it would be exactly what she'd wear when she next met Kaufman.

Chapter Forty-four

Spinks released Kal from custody in the early hours of the morning. Any earlier and intelligence might filter back to Raphael and place her under suspicion. There was no knowing how deep Raphael's networks infiltrated, but Kal was willing to bet they went pretty damn subterranean.

During the shoot-out, one officer received a gun-shot wound and he was in intensive care. The bullet came from Raphael's gun so he was facing serious charges.

The man half-beaten to death had refused the Cartel's lawyer and information was spilling from his lips. Kal wasn't so naïve to believe it would bring down the Cartel, but it would certainly put a dent in their activities and it would put Raphael away. Plus she'd blocked their attempts to ensnare her. It wasn't a bad night's work.

Walking towards the underground, she stretched her stiff shoulders. All night in the cell, she'd not been able to stop thinking about Sophie. She'd left Sophie alone with a promise she'd be home soon and the girl was close to a breakthrough. One more trip back to Lilac

Mansions and Sophie would remember everything, Kal was pretty certain of it.

When she got back to 701, it gave her a shock.

Sophie had left no note and there was no clue as to where she might be. Shit. Kal paced the lounge and found a suspicious mark on the floor behind the settee. What had happened? Goddammit – she'd wanted to be there to help when the memories came, because she felt sure that was what had happened – Sophie had remembered back to the night of her parents' death.

Where the hell would Sophie go? Who would she turn to? Kal paced, and the more she didn't know and the more she worried, the more she knew whose neck she wanted to get her hands around. She imagined squeezing the breath from him. Imagined inflicting pain.

Kal stormed from the apartment.

Raymond Kendrick wasn't expecting the intrusion. Kal smashed into his office and then smashed Kendrick against the wall.

'Where the hell is she!'

Kendrick shook his head and Kal followed up with a punch to his stomach. Hard enough to make him double over, but not enough to cause lasting damage.

'I said, where is she? And I'm not going to ask a third time.'

'I d-don't – I don't know.'

Kal stepped back and regarded him with cold eyes. She had no interest in beating up innocent people, except, of course, Kendrick wasn't innocent.

'You were her guardian, fuck it. And you *left* her. You left her to cope on her own. You miserable snivelling shit. You're not even a person, let alone a brother.'

She felt her arm tensing for a second strike and half-heartedly reeled it in, going for a neck grab and jerking Kendrick upright. Even though he was more than a head taller than her, Kendrick made no attempt to retaliate, which infuriated and disgusted her even further. He tried to speak and, under the squeeze of her hands, it came out like a gargle. Kal grabbed his lapels and pushed him against the desk.

'I – I know.'

'Know what, you bastard? All you're interested in is your money. Where is she?'

'I know what I did to Sophie was wrong. I know I'm a shitty brother. I should have been there. I should have been there that night, not out partying, then it might never have happened.'

'Your step-mother was attractive, wasn't she?'

'W-hat?'

'You heard ass-hole. Did you have the hots for her? Were you lovers?'

Kendrick had gone red to the roots of his hair. 'Certainly not!'

Sometimes you have to shake the tree until something falls out. And shake it hard. This was one of those times because she knew he'd not been Charlotte's lover.

'I think you're a lying little shit. You fucked your own step-mother and then she got bored with you. So you murdered her.'

Kendrick's eyes were falling out of their sockets. 'You're mad.'

'Talk or you're finished,' Kal said, in exactly the tone her father used which had chilled her blood.

Kendrick started blathering.

'That's insane. I never touched Charlie. It's out... out of the question. I didn't kill them. Listen, I know I've been shitty. I know Sophie deserved better. I should have been there for her. I've never been able to admit how badly I neglected her, right when she needed me.'

'Go on.'

'And she's been getting worse recently and her headaches getting out of control and Urwin getting so wound up about it.'

Kal's anger stopped dead in its tracks.

She held her breath. Dr Urwin Kaufman. Martin Kendrick's friend. It was the last piece of the puzzle, the one question she'd not been able to answer – why had the killer gone quiet? Now she knew the answer. He went quiet because he had his own Charlie. He had his very own little replacement right under his own roof.

Kal's back flashed hot.

'Get us to your car!' she shouted.

Chapter Forty-five

At Melrose Clinic, the two of them ran up the driveway.

Kal shouted at Kendrick. 'Find Kaufman.'

But Doctor Kaufman wasn't on the premises, and neither was Marty.

'Ms King checked out this morning,' the receptionist told Kal.

Shit, this was a dead end, and there was no thread to unravel, and it was her own fault for splitting her attention with Raphael when she should have been with her friends. She needed to find Sophie. And where the hell was Marty? What if Kaufman had taken her? A dread turned her guts cold. When she grabbed Kendrick's keys from him, his fingers felt hot and hers were ice.

As she ran out of the building, Kal heard a shout.

'Wait.'

It was a young man, one of the chess players she'd seen on her first visit. He caught up with her on the steps.

'If you're looking for that black woman, Dr Kaufman was with her yesterday. The doctor said she was dangerous. She was talking to my friend Seb, and he's gone missing too.'

Kal made herself stop and absorb the information. Seb was friends with Eliza and Sophie, so what was the connection? Why had Seb gone missing now? What if Seb was in danger? What if Kaufman had him? She must make crystal clear choices on priorities and it couldn't be Marty. Should she first track down Sophie? Or Seb?

'Raymond, call the police. Tell them Seb is missing.' She gave him Spinks' number.

'Where are you going? I want to come with you,' Raymond said, 'and help find my sister.'

'No, I need you here. Contact me with any news.'

Kal said it through gritted teeth. She must trust Spinks to find Seb, and it would leave her free to find Sophie. Once again, she must leave Marty on her own. She knew Marty would say she could fend for herself, and she knew Marty was right but it didn't stop Kal feeling responsible.

As Kal drove away, she did her best to push her best friend from her mind.

***

Kaufman's last words rang in Marty's ears.

'I've given you the same poison. If you don't get an antidote within twenty-four hours you'll both be dead.'

Kaufman had driven them to a deserted house in the countryside. Marty had bitten the inside of her mouth and pinched her arms to try to keep conscious, only she'd still missed chunks of the journey. She

250

remembered bouncing along a rutted track and the next thing, she and Seb were shoved into a basement and the door slammed shut.

They fell down the steps, and Marty grabbed Seb around the waist and wedged her body beneath him as they tumbled. She'd landed onto packed earth with Seb half on top of her.

Whatever Kaufman had pumped him with, Seb couldn't speak or move and his breathing was shallow. His lids kept closing. Shit, he was in a bad way. She had to get help. Seb was frail – he might have much less than twenty-four hours.

Marty was furious with herself for falling into Kaufman's trap. She would rip down the walls with her bare hands if she needed to. Anything to get the boy to safety.

The fall had torn the skin off both her knees. Like the biting and the pinching, the pain cleared her head a little. It must be working against whatever Kaufman injected her with. She must find a way to make it stronger and get her body to fight against the drugs.

Marty started doing push ups. She was breathless and the drugs made her clumsy but she managed twenty. Then she changed to sit ups. Twenty. Then back to push ups. Twenty-five. Then sit-ups. Thirty. It was working. The more she sweated the more her head cleared and her arms and legs got back to normal.

Marty checked Seb again. She felt certain his breathing rate had decreased and his eyes were now permanently closed. Shit.

The cellar door was firmly locked, and it was solid and showed no signs of weakness. Thick floorboards made up the ceiling and a small amount of light filtered through the cracks. Marty found a plank of wood in the corner and she banged systematically on each slat in the ceiling. But none of them showed signs of being loose.

The only other possible exit was a metal grille in the wall. A little above eye level, it was probably for ventilation. Marty hoped it would lead to the outside. It would be just about big enough to get through.

There was nothing to stand on and Marty used her arms to pull herself up, thanking her lucky stars she'd been working out daily for her recuperation. The little she could see told her nothing of where it led to. She would have to hope the gamble paid off because getting through it would take all her strength.

With the plank of wood, she set to work. The weakest point of the grille was where it was attached to the brickwork. She smashed at the edge, and little bits of brick crumbled away. *Pam, pam, pam.*

She allowed herself to rest only when her arms shook so much she couldn't hold the plank up any longer. Each time she had to drop it, Marty checked on Seb. She talked to him, massaging his cheeks and hands, both of which were growing cold. She started checking his heart and was sure it was getting weaker.

'Please don't die, Seb. You've got to hang on. I'm getting us out of here.'

Seb's decline spurred her on. She mustn't collapse. She must keep going. Thirst burned at the back of her throat. She ignored it. Ignored too the blisters on her hands which ripped away and started to bleed, and the giant splinters in her palms and the terrible ache in her shoulders and back.

After a good half hour of effort, the bricks at the bottom released the grille but she couldn't get it free at the top, nor at the sides. Damn it, she couldn't take the strain any more.

Marty crouched panting and she wiped the sweat out of her eyes. If she could release it on one side, she'd have a chance of kicking it in if she could manage to haul herself up there.

Seb's skin was getting clammy. What if he was slipping into a coma? What if his heart gave out? What if Kaufman was telling the truth, and there was some kind of toxin working its way through Seb's body? What if he died before she had chance to – No, she mustn't think like that. She had to keep going. But Marty knew her stamina was spent. She couldn't keep going any longer. She must get up there and give it everything she had left.

Marty retied strips from her hospital gown around her hands. They were soaked with blood. She did it slowly, gathering her strength for the final push.

'This is it, Seb,' she said. 'Wish me luck.'

Taking a deep breath, she reached up with both hands and took a firm grip on the grille. She pulled herself up until her body weight rested awkwardly on the sill of the brickwork. She'd have one chance and if it didn't work, the force from her own strike would propel her back onto the floor of the basement – which would likely injure her. If it worked, she'd go with the force of her own kick through the opening, hoping not to hurt herself in any fall, should the opening prove to let out onto a drop. And hoping not to get ripped to shreds if the grille remained attached at the top. The odds weren't encouraging. Don't think about it, Marty told herself. Just do it.

Chapter Forty-six

Sophie dipped her brush in water and chose sky blue to finish the detail. It reminded her of summer days. It also reminded Sophie of her mother. She swallowed and then finished the butterfly wings.

The makeup brush clattered onto her childhood dresser and Sophie twisted her shoulder and admired the trail of tiny butterflies sweeping up over her shoulder. In the dim glow of the bedroom lamp, the sequins of her silver dress reflected the blue of the butterflies' wings.

Sophie swept her clutch purse from the bed and walked along the top landing, pausing for a moment at the top of the staircase and then descending. She would take a tour of the garden first, and inhale the night scents of honeysuckle and roses and explain to her mother she was doing this for her.

When Sophie came back in the house, she went straight to her little landing where she sat down to wait.

The house was quiet. Sophie leant against the balustrade and another memory surfaced, this time without pain, of Kaufman in his balaclava walking out of the house and leaving the front door open. She'd run as fast as she could to her bedroom and hidden in the big wooden box under the window. That's where the policeman found her.

Sophie remembered his voice and how she'd trembled when his hand reached in to touch her cheek. She hadn't cried when he lifted her out. She hadn't said a word, just stared at his nice, kind eyes and then she'd been pressed against his jacket all the way down the stairs. She was glad about that now, because she understood how little Sophie *knew* and little Sophie didn't want to see the blood and the bodies.

In the back of the car, they'd wrapped her in a blanket and the policeman sat next to her, though he didn't say anything. Later on, at the police station, a woman had given her a teddy bear and told Sophie her parents were dead.

Sophie sat on the step, waiting for Kaufman. On her lap lay Penny's clutch purse, and inside it, were the syringe, pepper spray and knife.

Chapter Forty-seven

I told you Charlotte Kendrick liked to play games and how she enjoyed her clandestine activities as a call girl which no one knew about except me. I never let on. And I let her live and indulged my urges with other targets. I even manoeuvred myself to become a colleague of the husband she chose and I'd like to think he saw me as a friend, though of course, that was simply his stupidity. I was far from a friend.

Over the years, I kept regular contact with my angel, and every time I saw Charlie after the release of killing a target, it gave me a thrill. It was as if she silently celebrated with me. As if my angel shone down on me and acknowledged my mastery over life and death. In her eyes, I saw how she enjoyed it as much as I did. I could see it in her smile. In her lips. In her lovely, almond eyes. It was a silent communication between two linked souls. Her silent blessing of my activities. Her silent acknowledgement of the ones I killed for her.

So I suppose you want to know why I had to end her?

You see it all went wrong and I didn't even see it coming.

One day when I went to see Charlie she told me she'd decided to put an end to her secret life. She told me we couldn't meet any more. She wanted to confess to her husband she'd been unfaithful and she hoped he would forgive her. Of course he would. The man was besotted with Charlotte. He would give her the moon if he was able.

It was unthinkable and I could not allow her to do it. I could not lose her. And I could not lose the hold I had over her which was all wrapped up in her secrets and the lies she liked to tell.

After that meeting, I could barely sleep.

I was soon invited for drinks by Martin and in one glance I saw how Charlotte had transformed. She no longer looked at me like an accomplice. Naturally, she had no knowledge of my activities, but I knew in my heart that she knew. And now I was suddenly an outsider. Now she looked at me coldly.

And that's when I took the gun from my pocket.

***

Seb made a horrible gurgling sound, and Marty clenched her muscles. With a roar, she let fly a mighty kick. Her soles hit the grille full force and it flew away at the bottom where she'd worked it loose. Then it ripped away on both sides, so her legs flew out into space. She didn't try to stop them. Marty let her body follow her legs through the opening, trying to slow herself down by grabbing onto the brickwork.

The grille remained attached at a top corner and so it ripped her skin off as she scraped through. Her head banged on the brickwork. She didn't care. She felt her legs in space and then she fell.

Marty lay dazed. She'd landed on a bank covered in weeds. She stared up at clouds in a blue sky. She'd made it. She was free.

The house was surrounded by farmland. She could hear a low drone – the sound of a distant car – which meant there was a road nearby.

Twenty minutes later, Marty walked along the edge of a field with Seb over her shoulder. It hadn't been easy getting back inside the cellar, but she'd found something to stand on and managed to crawl back through the opening.

In the daylight, the boy looked close to death. When Marty finally flagged down a car, the couple who stopped were horrified. They took them straight to the nearest accident and emergency.

'He's been poisoned,' Marty told the medical staff. 'Injected with something toxic.'

Once her own hands were bandaged and she'd been given clothes, Marty waited outside for LeeMing. It wasn't long before she heard the sound of his motorbike, and he wasted no time in asking questions. LeeMing handed her a helmet and Marty got on the back and the two of them made straight for Lilac Mansions.

***

Kaufman gripped the steering wheel. The dreamers like Sophie and Eliza were always easy to work with. They were so susceptible to auto-suggestion, or hypnosis, as people liked to call it. Whereas Marty King was grounded and far too practically minded. She would have been impossible to subdue. He'd come back and deal with her and the boy later.

In fact, Sophie had been one of his easiest patients to control. She drank in his autosuggestion like a baby draws in milk.

From the beginning, she'd been a mini-version of Charlotte, with her almond eyes and wistful expression. The older Sophie got, the more she resembled her mother, which made Kaufman's time with Sophie even more enchanting. In fact, their weekly consultations at Melrose were the highlight of his life. Kaufman knew why Arthur Connell had been speechless the first time he'd seen Sophie – because it had been like walking into a room and finding Charlotte there.

When Kaufman received Sophie's call at the clinic, he knew their time was up.

'Meet me at my parent's house,' was all Sophie said.

'Of course, my dear,' Kaufman replied.

He put down the phone and reached to the tube of orange-scented cream. He moisturised his hands and nodded to himself. 'And today, you will take your mother's place and look at me for the last time with the eyes of an angel.'

Chapter Forty-eight

The door of Lilac Mansions was open and Kaufman saw Charlie and Sophie sitting on the stairs.

'Hello, my dear.'

'Stay exactly where you are,' Sophie said.

It looked like the girl's memory had returned. He could see a change in her. There was a hardness in her face. And there was rage and anger knotted inside her.

He'd been fighting a losing battle against it happening these last months. Finishing Penny and then Eliza to stop Sophie leaving him hadn't been enough. And yet Sophie was still so predictable, so like her little friend, Eliza, who'd been trusting right until the end – so easy to manipulate and play with. Kaufman licked his lips.

'I'm much stronger now,' Sophie said.

'Of course you are.' Kaufman nodded. 'And you are so much like your mother.'

'Is that why you haven't killed me yet?'

'Goodness, what an imagination you have. I suppose you won't believe me but it's the truth that Eliza took her own life.'

'No. You knew my memories kept trying to come back. I was slipping from your control. And Penny and

261

Eliza were helping me leave Melrose. You kept me weak all these years and you killed my mother. You shot my father. You're a murdering, evil monster.'

'You're fragile, Sophie. You have a frail disposition and you need care. It's nothing to be ashamed of.'

'Shut up! All those drugs you had me on. It was *you* who kept me weak. You're the one who *kept me frail*. And all along you murdered my parents!'

Kaufman slowly shook his head. 'You haven't been on any real medication for years, only dummy drugs. It wasn't me who kept you weak, you did it to yourself.'

That got to her. Kaufman saw how he'd created a tiny sliver of doubt. He was breaking down her resolve already. This was child's play. She was so easy. Soon she'd crumple like a stack of cards.

'Come now, my dear, I can explain everything.' And Kaufman took a few steps across the hallway.

'I said stay where you are.'

The girl's voice was steely and it made Kaufman pause. He would never have expected her to gain so much strength in so little time away from him. That was the trouble when people slipped from your grasp. He pressed his lips together.

Kaufman was standing next to Charlie's flower mural and her ran his fingers over the blue and purple flowers.

'Charlie was a gifted artist.' He stared straight at Sophie. 'And a prostitute.'

Sophie laughed. 'Oh, don't think you can shake me so easily. I've known about that for years. Is it why you killed her? Did she turn you down?'

Kaufman clenched his fists. 'Charlotte knew what I was and she was the only one who knew! She could see it in my soul.'

'Could see what you were? What? A twisted killer? And you're the one who calls *me* sick? You're one hell of a sadistic bastard. My mother would've been the first to turn you in if she'd known–'

Kaufman held up his hand to interrupt her. 'I've got Seb.'

That hit her – slammed her straight between the eyes as if he'd smacked her against a wall. He enjoyed the horror.

'You're lying.'

Sophie said it with bravado, with her chin up, and he smiled again at how she tried to hide her doubts.

'I've a video of him unconscious. I've injected him with poison and If he doesn't get the anti-dote, he'll die.'

Kaufman held out his phone and climbed the first few steps of the stairs. On the screen was a video of Seb, his face ashen, drool running down his chin. The sound of Seb's laboured breathing filled the space between them.

'Keep away!'

He ignored her. 'Everything I tell you is true, Sophie. If you come back with me to Melrose, I promise everything will be all right. I'll let Seb go and you and I will go back to how we were before.'

Now he was close enough for her to see the video.

'No, no, not Seb, you can't kill him.'

As Sophie's hand flew to her mouth, Kaufman started to talk to her in a low voice, in the special way he'd cultured during their years in the consultation room. In auto-suggestion, the tone is as important at the words. Yet Kaufman knew too which words would slip through Sophie's defences and build her anxiety. He knew how to press the button which started her panicking. And the right words to make her crumble inside. Kaufman could make her so helpless she'd need to reach out to her doctor for help. And, of course, her doctor would be there. As he spoke, Kaufman crept up the stairs.

Sophie pressed her hands over her ears. The bastard had Seb. Please no, that couldn't be true. But what if it was? What if Seb was right now lying somewhere barely breathing? What if Kaufman had already killed him? Kaufman was coming up the stairs. She could see his shiny shoes on the red carpet, just like she'd seen them all those years ago, getting closer.

Sophie shook her head to try to get rid of Kaufman's voice. It was getting inside her head. No, it *was* inside her head. It was the voice which always invaded her mind. Kaufman's lips moved, yet his voice sounded inside her. How could that be? No! She had nowhere to go. Nowhere to hide. His horrible voice was right inside her drowning out her own thoughts.

'Everything will be fine. Come back with me to Melrose and everything will be all right.'

Sophie thought of the pepper spray. She thought of reaching her hand inside the purse and she really wanted to but she couldn't move and then… Kaufman stood in front of her and she tried to speak, tried to ask him about Seb.

'Shhhh,' Kaufman said with a smile, his index finger on his lips. 'Come with me and everything will be all right.'

Sophie tried to slip her hand into the purse but her arm wouldn't move and she was shaking too much. Her mind had turned to jelly. Her thoughts were crumbling and nothing made sense. What could she do except surrender? Give up. Kaufman had always been stronger. Always been able to dominate her. Make her think as he wanted. Make her do as he wanted. Tears rolled down Sophie's cheeks, and instead of her hand moving to her purse, it rose up to meet Kaufman's, and she allowed her doctor to take her hand.

***

Kal hardly saw the road as she drove to Lilac Mansions with her foot pressed down to the floor.

Dr Urwin Kaufman of Melrose Clinic. Of course. The man who'd had Sophie under his power all this time. A doctor who knew Martin and Charlotte Kendrick and who'd undoubtedly murdered them in their own house. And who'd brutally butchered Penny and then killed Eliza because he wanted to keep Sophie under his control. A sociopathic killer who'd been stalking women for decades. The evil murderer whom she'd sent her best friend, alone, to check out. Kal's heart was thumping so hard the sound filled the car.

Parking at the end of the road, she approached Lilac Mansions on foot. When she saw a car standing on the front driveway, the hairs on her arms stood on end – Kaufman, she presumed. The fucker. Which meant he was inside. Was Sophie inside too? Who had arrived first? What was happening in there? Was Kaufman after Sophie? Or was Sophie after Kaufman?

Kal followed the glowing line of night lights to the front door. There were no sounds, only the silence of the night and damp, countryside air. No house lights were on.

She cursed. What if Sophie decided to take things into her own hands? Why else would Sophie have left 701? And why else would she come back here alone, except to face the killer? Kal shivered. She must be stealthy. She must be silent – not a twig, not a crunch of gravel, no giveaway grate of a shoe – no man-made noise must alert them she was coming. Kal felt herself go cool and calm inside.

At the back of the house, a first-floor bathroom gave a way in. The window had a circular ventilation vent and Kal climbed a nearby lilac tree to reach it. She had no silent cutting gear nor the suction pads her father used to infiltrate a building. Instead, she tapped a stone around the plastic, cursing at the way the noise travelled, until she heard the glass surround giving way.

If she was unlucky the vent would land in a bath and the sound would ricochet and bring Kaufman running. She punched it through. The vent flew into the room and skittered across the tiled floor. She waited, alert to any sign it had given her away. After a few moments, she reached her arm through the round hole and undid the window catch.

No gun, no equipment – what did that leave her with as an advantage? Kung fu skills with a leg which didn't function as well as it should? The element of surprise? It didn't feel like it would be enough. *Cunning*, whispered the voice in her head. In her father's coaching sessions, she'd excelled at cunning, surpassing even him – yes, that would give her an edge. She trod carefully along the top floor landing.

The top floor lay in darkness, with the only light filtering up from the downstairs lounge. Descending the staircase she'd be fully exposed – too bad, she'd have to take the chance. Kal ran down the stairs, careful not to miss her footing, her steps masked by the thick carpet.

Getting down on her stomach, she crawled across the hallway. The door of the lounge was half open and she positioned herself to peer through the crack between the hinges and the frame. It gave a narrow angle of vision. First of the near wall. Then of the window to the garden and a sofa. She adjusted her body a third time and saw the end of the room and a sight which made the breath catch in her throat.

Sophie reclined on a chaise longue. Only the girl's head and torso were visible but nothing about her looked right. Her face appeared frozen and waxy. Worse than that, Sophie's blonde hair fanned out around her face in a perfect arrangement. Shit. And that look on her face meant chemical influence. The back of a man came in and out of Kal's view as he bent over Sophie, and Sophie stared skyward into his face. She couldn't see Sophie's eyes, but she was sure they would be full of terror.

Kal tensed, ready to charge straight in. Except she stopped herself, because the man's hand came into view and he held a scalpel. Kal stared at the silver blade as Kaufman waved it backwards and forwards in front of Sophie's face.

Her muscles twitched. Kaufman could plunge it into Sophie and kill her in an instant. As soon as he realised there was an intruder he could strike before Kal reached the chaise longue. Her back was covered in sweat. Kaufman must mean to slice off Sophie's eyelids as he'd done with his other victims and Sophie seemed unable to move. No, she couldn't take him in an attack, she must lure him away from Sophie.

***

That night at Lilac Mansions, when I took the gun from my pocket, Martin was confused. I suppose he couldn't understand why one of his best friends would draw a weapon in his own house.

I saw disbelief on his face and then anger. He started shouting at me as if he thought his intellect would be sufficient to win superiority. How idiotic. Charlotte was quicker to understand the danger, though I closed my ears to her pleading. I killed Martin with one shot to the chest. Bang.

Of course, I'd meant to make Charlie into a wonderful and final, angelic symbol and I had the scalpel in my pocket. But those lovely almond eyes were looking at me with such loathing I fell into a blind rage. I set at her with the blade.

As I stabbed her again and again, Charlie dragged herself across the carpet towards her dead husband. It so enraged me how she wished to be close to him, I lost all control until she lay silent in a pool of blood, unable to reach him in her dying moments.

It would have been over then if it hadn't been for the girl on the stairs. The girl with the same almond eyes as her mother and who looked at me with such innocence and terror. I knew then I would do everything in my power to cultivate her. Until the time came for her to take Charlotte's place.

Kaufman gazed at Sophie lying prone on the chaise longue. He stroked her golden hair fanned out on the cushions.

'You look so much like her, did you know that? It was a comfort having you at the clinic. Every day I could see her in your eyes.'

Yes, Kaufman wanted Charlies' eyes fixed on him in death. He'd been robbed of that once and he wouldn't let it happen again.

Chapter Forty-nine

Kal squirmed backwards across the hallway and then raced up the stairs to exit the bathroom the way she'd come.

Outside, cold air chilled the sweat on her back.

She was wearing a denim jacket and a tight V-neck tunic over black leggings. Taking off the leggings, she stuffed them under a bush. The V-neck tunic reached to mid-thigh. Kal went back to the front door.

Knock. Knock.

'Sophie,' Kal called, 'it's me, Kal. Are you in there?'

She knocked again. 'Soph open up, it's freezing out here. Are you okay? The girls sent me.'

Kal hopped from one leg to the other. Should Kaufman be stupid enough to answer the door, he'd zoom in on her bare legs and it would give more traction to her story. Except he didn't. Instead he spoke to her over an intercom.

'This is private property. What exactly do you think you're doing?'

'Who the hell are you?' she said.

'My name is Dr Kaufman.'

'Yeah, too right,' Kal said, pulling out her phone. 'I don't know who the hell you are and this place belongs to my friend Sophie.'

She made as if to dial. Likely he'd have a security camera trained on her and he'd presume she was calling the police.

'Wait! I'm Sophie's doctor, she's under my care.'

'Soph doesn't have a doctor.'

'I'm her psychiatrist. Perhaps you'd better come in and Sophie can speak for herself.'

There was a click and the door snapped off the latch. Kal walked into the hallway.

'Where are you Soph?'

Kaufman called from the lounge. 'She's in here.'

He'd angled the chaise longue away from the doorway.

Kal saw Kaufman taking her in with one glance. He was ordinary looking, of average height, average build, average everything with neat, dark hair and a narrow, trimmed beard. A man you'd easily overlook. The worst killers were always that type.

'How did you get here?' Kaufman asked.

'Taxi of course. And my name's Kal.'

'It's kind of you to check on your friend. Rather a long way to come though, isn't it?'

Kaufman was sitting in a huge arm chair right beside Sophie. And he was suspicious. Good for him.

'I didn't have much choice. Candice sent me and Candice isn't someone I argue with.'

'Candice, oh yes,' Kaufman said, nodding. 'Sophie mentioned her on occasion. Well please come in, though I can't allow you to stay long. Sophie is resting.'

The scalpel was out of sight but Kaufman was close enough to Sophie to be able to use it to severely injure her. So Kal kept up the pretence nothing was wrong. All she could see so far was Sophie's hand trailing on the carpet and a sequin clutch purse lying close by.

She walked around the chaise longue and came to a stop staring at Sophie. The girl's eyes were open and she was looking straight at Kal.

'What the hell's going on?' Kal said.

Kaufman was sitting very still, observing her. *Too still*, she thought. What the hell was he playing at?

She shook Sophie's arm. 'Hey, are you okay?'

'She can't respond.'

Kal backed off a few steps. 'What the hell have you done to her?'

Come on Kaufman, move away.

'Exactly how good a friend are you of Sophie's?'

She didn't like the tone of his voice. It was too calm and too smooth. He pulled his hand out of his pocket and in it he held a syringe. Kal judged the distance between them. At least he wasn't armed with the scalpel, so she could jump him and he wouldn't be able to hurt Sophie.

'In case you're thinking about it, I don't advise you to attack me. You see this fluid?' Kaufman tapped the syringe with his fingertip. 'It's an antidote. And I only have one dose.'

Her back flashed hot. *What the hell—*

'If you run away or if you attack me I'll pull out the plunger and the antidote will be lost. Without it your friend will die.'

The sick bastard, he was playing games with her. The problem being he might be telling the truth. Then again, she knew one of his weak points.

'I'm a prostitute.'

He was staring at her legs. 'I was hoping you might be. Now pull the settee around to face Sophie and lie down on it.'

'Wh-what do you want? What are you going to do? What have you done to Sophie!'

He held the syringe in mid-air, keeping his hand on the plunger. 'Do as I say. And remember, if you run, or if you try anything, Sophie will never get this antidote and she will die.'

She dragged the settee as instructed, taking her time so she could think through her strategy. She felt sure he was lying about the antidote. Surely he'd injected Sophie with the same drug he'd used on his other victims, to subdue her for the cutting? There'd been no mention of a toxin on any of the post mortem reports. Then again, a number of neurotoxins broke down in the body and would be reported as an anaesthetic on an autopsy analysis.

'It doesn't have to be like this,' she said. 'If it's sex you want…'

He slowly shook his head. 'Lie down.'

She must rely on her own judgement of him. Kaufman was clearly mad. And he relied on his mind. He was trying to manipulate her into a position of extreme weakness. He wanted her to voluntarily lie down so he could do god knows what to her. All by him planting the idea that if she did otherwise Sophie would die. Yet she was certain the syringe wasn't an antidote. Kaufman was a master manipulator and it was time to call his bluff.

In one movement, she leapt for Kaufman. He fell like a sack of potatoes and she punched him in the side of the head. She wanted him to fight back. It would give her an excuse to really hurt him but he didn't even try. Kaufman was soft and doughy and an easy target.

Kal fought her own desire to pummel him to a pulp. He deserved it. Kaufman was a monster. She could give him permanent brain damage – he would be a vegetable for life, or she could break every bone in his body, or she could– Sophie made a gurgling noise.

In a couple of steps Kal was at Sophie's side. Sophie was trying to speak and Kal massaged her hands and her arms and her face. Getting her circulation going was ridding Sophie's system of whatever shit Kaufman had put into her. Kal massaged her legs and Sophie started wiggling her toes.

It was then that Kal felt a jab at her ankle. She looked down to see Kaufman looking up at her. The bastard had jabbed her with the syringe. Kal felt sure she'd kicked it well out of range. For a moment time stood still, and then she felt a numbness in her feet.

'You son of a b-!'

She started throttling him. Kaufman's face went purple. His eyes bulged and his tongue stuck out. But Kal could feel the poison spreading up her legs and she fell to her knees, on top of Kaufman. She must end it. Cursing, she fought to get a hold on the pressure point which would finish him off. But her fingers were going numb and she had no grip. She understood the danger. Understood she'd been compromised.

Kaufman had a look of triumph.

'Sophie!' she screamed. 'Get out, Sophie. Get out.'

Kaufman was struggling to his feet, winded and wounded by her earlier blows, but not out for the count. By now, she was slumped on the carpet, unable to get up.

Kaufman coughed and rubbed at his neck. 'It's fast acting, isn't it?' he said. 'Your entire musculature will be paralysed in a matter of moments, you bitch.'

The twisted, evil piece of fucking sh–.

Kaufman kicked her in the stomach.

Sophie was struggling on the chaise longue. She tried to stand and her legs buckled. Kaufman bent over Sophie drinking in her terror.

'That's it, my dear, that's exactly what I want. Be terrified. Because I am your master and I shall make you my creation.'

Kaufman was completely psychotic. Kal was on the floor and fast losing control of her muscles and it was all she could do to propel herself with her knees and elbows and drag herself towards Sophie inch by inch. It was a deep pile carpet and that made it worse. Only extreme force of will kept her moving.

Sophie could see Kal dragging herself across the floor. Kaufman had told her how Charlotte had dragged herself towards her dead husband in her dying moments. For Sophie it was bitter-sweet – her mother might have married her father for money but she'd ended up loving him. Now Kal was grunting with the effort just as her mother must have done. It was then Sophie spied her sequin purse.

'Run Sophie!'

Kal knew if she could just get closer, she'd be in reach of Kaufman. He was ignoring her now, she could make it. She had to make it.

Sophie was trying to push to her knees and, in the distance, Kal felt sure she could hear the sound of a motorbike. For a moment, she wondered if it might be her father. No, that was stupid, her father was dead.

She was running out of strength; the injection was claiming her. No! She wouldn't let it. Kaufman was bending over Sophie, and Sophie cringed, pulling away from him.

'Get away from her, you bastard!'

He had his scalpel, he was going to cut her. He was moving in close.

Kal made a final lunge for Kaufman's ankle. It was then she heard the *hiss* of a spray and Kaufman screamed and recoiled. He staggered backwards, covering his eyes with his hands.

Right in front of Kal, Kaufman fell writhing and shrieking.

Sophie tossed aside the perfume and pepper spray and groped for Kaufman's scalpel. And the girl raised it high and plunged it deep into Kaufman's neck.

***

By the time Marty and LeeMing smashed their way into the house, Kaufman lay dead on the golden carpet.

Chapter Fifty

Marty sat on the end of Kal's bed.

'The doctor says you can go home,' Marty said. 'And the police have finished questioning Sophie. Kaufman died of blood loss from a severed jugular and they'll propose it was self-defence on Sophie's part.'

Kal nodded.

'You and LeeMing arrived in time to pick up the pieces, but Marty, you should have checked into hospital with Seb. What if Kaufman hadn't been lying about the poison? You took a huge risk.'

'And so what? You think you're the only one who can take chances?' Marty said it with a shrug. 'Besides, I was pretty sure it was bullshit given how the effect wore off after a couple of hours sweating in that damn cellar.'

'I'm sorry I sent you to check out Kaufman on your own – I mean, given he turned out to be a homicidal maniac and all. Kaufman should have come up on my radar way sooner.'

'You're brilliant Kal but you're not a genius, so I don't think so. He was a clever bastard and he'd evaded justice for years. You can't cover all the bases on your own and if there's one thing I've learned in the last twenty-four hours – being a lone wolf like your father doesn't work. You need full-time back-up.'

Kal gave her friend a hard stare.

'Hang on, that sounds like a proposal. I thought you hated what I do?'

'I never hated it. It's just I was never sure of your tactics. Now I realise when you're dealing with scum like Kaufman, your way might be the only way. Not knowing if I'd be able to get Seb help in time, it changed the way I see things. So, if you can put up with me keeping you in line, I want in.'

Kal laughed. 'Sounds great and I wouldn't want it any other way. Partner.'

Chapter Fifty-one

Six months later

Sophie spent weeks planning the mural. She wanted to put in a little touch for everyone and in a coded way so only she would know what it all represented.

For her mother, she painted a garland of purple and blue lilacs. Amongst the lilacs she placed one red rose, fully opened, which was Charlotte's love for Martin.

For her father, Sophie put in a red ribbon trailing through the stars. It was a symbol of his staircase in his house of dreams.

Eliza was in there and Penny too. The more difficult one to choose for was Kal, but Sophie was pleased with her final choice.

***

Kal tried not to laugh when Raymond Kendrick almost dropped a tray of food. At least he was trying and that was what mattered. The housewarming was in full swing and a big banner hung on the wall, "Congratulations Sophie, Seb and Wayne".

Sophie had bought her own apartment and Seb, and Wayne the chess-player, were her flat mates. A photograph of Eliza sat on the side and Kal tried hard not to stare at it. She didn't want to be tearful in front of all these people.

They'd all admired Sophie's stunning mural. It started in the hallway and went all the way up the stairs. Kal had especially liked the lone wolf on the mountain top. It seemed to survey the scene below, like a guardian. Sophie had laughed. 'I thought you might like that,' was all she said.

Arthur Connell proposed a toast and they raised their glasses. 'To new beginnings, and… absent friends.'

Kal put her arm around Sophie. Marty had her hand on Seb's shoulder and over in the corner, someone turned up the music and a bunch of nurses from Melrose started dancing. LeeMing pulled Sophie into the centre with him.

'Are you coming for a dance, Kal?' LeeMing's girlfriend asked.

'In a few minutes,' Kal said.

'Sure and, hey, I wanted to tell you, you did a great job. I can see why Lee thinks so much of you.'

Kal shrugged. 'Thanks.'

Marty came over carrying two glasses. 'You okay?'

Kal drained her glass and accepted a new one. She took a big swig from it and she knew they were both thinking about Eliza. 'Of course I am.'

'Seems like you're getting on better with Fiona.'

'That's a bit of an exaggeration, but yeah, as friend's girlfriends go, she's not so bad.'

Marty smiled. 'That's something I thought I'd never hear you say.'

Kal took another sip. Sophie wasn't the only one who'd changed. Helping Sophie had helped Kal feel a bit more normal. It made her feel good about herself for the first time in a long time.

Marty chinked her glass against Kal's. 'You were spot on about Sophie – she's a strong kid. Something tells me she's going to make it, and don't forget I'm a real partner in these cases of yours from now on. Here's to bringing down more scum.'

Earlier on Kal caught up with Spinks. She told him working as his informant seemed like the right thing to do. She felt at home in the underworld, mingling with the murderers and the serial killers and the slime of London. Kaufman and Raphael were the tip of the iceberg. The underbelly of the city – what she liked to call London noir – was crawling with perpetrators just like them and that's exactly where she could make a difference.

'It's a deal, Marty. The next case we work together.'

'Yeah, you'd better make sure of it.' Marty was giving her a strange look. 'And something tells me you've already got some plans in that strategic head of yours.'

'I'll let you know,' Kal said and she laughed.

Kal watched Sophie dancing. She should thank Sophie for showing how life could go on, despite tragedy – how a survivor becomes strong. Inspired by Sophie, Kal hoped one day to find the person who'd survived her father's last assassination and hoped one day she'd have the courage to look that person in the eye and apologise. Yes, one day, but not today.

****

The Beauty Killers (Kal Medi book 3)

Women will go missing. And none will return.
A collector who lures women,
And then keeps them.

A string of beautiful women go missing.
And when an undercover policewoman disappears, Kal
and Marty take the case.

They track a killer who lures women, captures them and
keeps them.

But it soon becomes clear the case is even more sinister
than they imagined.

A high-level detective is linked to a cover-up and Kal
and Marty are caught in a complex,
evil conspiracy.
The clock is ticking to find the missing women and it
seems the perpetrator has more than one accomplice…

Chapter One

The walls are covered with photographs.

All our guests, past and present, stare back at me from rows of coloured, glossy squares. I like being surrounded by their beauty.

We have four guest rooms. At the moment, two of our rooms are empty, and it's my job to put that right.

Let me tell you about the last guest who checked out – she was blonde and she had lovely, long, glossy hair. Her performance on our catwalk was one of my favourites. Unfortunately, my Brother didn't feel the same way and he has more say in things than I do.

I work as the scout.

I'd picked that blonde out after weeks, no maybe months, of searching. Once she'd been selected, we lured her in. Then we kept her in one of our guest rooms. In the end her hair began falling out in handfuls. It was such a shame and she became so ugly the decision was made to get rid of her. What a pity after all those years of enjoyment.

Since her exit, our remaining two guests are behaving impeccably – so that's a bonus.

Anyway, I've been told to vary the game plan. Again we want a blonde and this time we want a specimen with more staying power. I've been scouting, and here's the good news – I've spotted a possible. Let's see what the others have to say about her. I think they'll be pleased.

Grab your copy of The Beauty Killers today!

Good Girl Bad Girl (Kal Medi book 1)

The darkest crimes can't stay hidden forever

A dead journalist?
A dead matron of a children's home
A young body washed up by the river

And a crime so evil it defies belief

The twisted killer is a man of power and influence.
A man who believes himself beyond the reach of the law.
His Achilles heel - a thirst for revenge that spans generations.

Only one person can nail him - Kal Medi – and she's the daughter of a criminal.

Kal Medi trusts no one and least of all Detective Inspector Spinks.
She's always hidden the fact her father was a criminal and he trained her to follow in his footsteps.

But when her journalist mother goes missing, Kal takes on the investigation.

Murder, trafficking and dark family secrets - she'll be forced to confront her own worst nightmares, to nail a twisted killer.

The first in the Kal Medi series.
Grab your copy today.

Good Girl Bad Girl is an ERIC HOFFER BOOK AWARD FINALIST 2017 and a READERS' FAVOURITE Five Star Book.

Prologue

Alesha could no longer feel her legs.

They hung, freezing and lifeless beneath the surface of the water. Tied above her head, Alesha's wrists rubbed raw against the restraints. No point in struggling. She tried that already, for hours or was it days? All the panic and the terror had long since run out of her and coursed down her legs.

And the pool deepened. When the water lapped her bellybutton, the flesh on Alesha's stomach contracted. Her two tormentors had climbed a ladder to escape, and a faint light drifted down from their exit route. Alesha watched the gleam of the rungs as they disappeared one by one beneath the inky blue.

How many times had she endured it? Twice, she thought, or was it three times? Each submersion, they stripped away her strength. Each time she was left with less of her self. They were paring her down layer by layer. Perhaps this time she'd be down to bare bones and the last shreds of will. Or perhaps this time she wouldn't make it.

Alesha shuddered as the water climbed her rib cage. Once it reached the level of her heart, she'd only have a few moments before she drowned. The dread rose up. She tried not to think about the moments ahead, pushing away the thought of them resuscitating her, then closing in for the interrogation, their violence and their voices filling every cell in her body.

Lapping at the sides of the chamber, the water sounded like gentle waves at the seaside. Alesha pressed her eyes closed. She wouldn't crack. She'd never tell them. They'd have to kill her first. The thought almost made her laugh. Yes, she'd wondered about that too, wondered if she were losing her mind. Thing is, if she were dead she wouldn't be able to give anything away. So perhaps she shouldn't fight it. Maybe it'd be better to take that one last breath as deep as she could and hope her heart gave out. Then the water would take away her secrets.

As the water rose, Alesha pushed deep inside her own mind and she saw her husband, his eyes full of life and he was young, like he'd been when they first met. He smiled at her. And the water reached her throat.

Now she could see her daughter, Kal, running with her black hair streaming out in the wind. At first, Kal

288

was a little girl laughing, and then she was a fiery teenager, and then she became a young woman. Alesha took a deep breath and sealed her lips closed. Kal wasn't smiling, she was shouting and determined and running towards Alesha. Alesha knew Kal'd never reach her in time. The water covered Alesha's nose and she felt the air expanding in her chest. Fight against it, she commanded herself. Don't take a breath. Her body thrashed and jerked. They'd turn the water off soon. Then they'd bring her back from the brink. Then they'd start again. Alesha felt a deep regret for handing her daughter a death sentence. Then she blacked out.

Praise for Good Girl Bad Girl

'A cracking read'
Amazon reviewer

'A taut, exciting thriller which had me hooked'
Reviewer, The Book Club TBC

"On the edge of my seat..."
Amazon reviewer

"A great suspenseful thriller written beautifully."
thecoffeeandkindle blogspot

"A real kick-ass heroine and a great lead character..."
Grab This Book

"...A thriller that will keep you up at night."
The Serial Reader

'Dangerous territory for exploration in a first novel...This is a terrific start for an author who demonstrates strong promise. 5 stars."
Hall of Fame, Top 100 reviewer, Vine Voice

"An action packed thriller with a strong, independent female character … A very well written book which will keep you hooked until the end. I look forward to reading the next in the series."
Reviewer, The Book Club TBC

"… multi-layered psychological thriller, I really enjoyed *Good Girl Bad Girl* and look forward to reading the next Kal Medi book."
BloominBrilliant Books

'Full of suspenseful twists and turns'
Amazon reviewer

Grab your copy of Good Girl Bad Girl today!

A note from Ann Girdharry

I hope you enjoyed *London Noir* and I'd like to say a huge thank you for choosing it.

London Noir is the second instalment and Kal and Marty have other adventures in store and other difficulties and challenges to face. I hope you enjoy reading about them as much as I like writing their stories.

Please leave a written review for *London Noir*, for instance, on Amazon. They really help me and they help others to discover my stories. Or maybe you can recommend *London Noir* to your friends and family...

My Reader's Group

If you'd like to keep up to date on my new releases join my **Reader's Group**. I shall send everyone on my list a note when my next book is published and let you know of any early 'read and review' opportunities.

(Don't worry, no spam, I promise.)

I usually offer a welcoming gift to new members of my Reader's Group, at the moment it's my Chilling

Tales of the Unexpected Boxed Set. You can find details on my webpage – www.girdharry.com

Kind regards,
Ann Girdharry

Connect with me on social media –
follow on Goodreads *www.goodreads.com/AnnGirdharry*
follow on Bookbub www.bookbub.com/profile/ann-girdharry
follow my Facebook Author page
https://www.facebook.com/AnnGirdharryAuthor/

My website *www.girdharry.com*

Acknowledgements

A good beta reader is like gold dust. Abbie Rutherford, Mark B., Mary Beth Marquis and Kath Middleton – your honest comments and insightful feedback have been so valuable. Thank you for helping me bring Kal, Marty, and this story, to life.

Titles by Ann Girdharry

Kal Medi series

Good Girl Bad Girl
London Noir
The Beauty Killers

Chilling Tales of the Unexpected
Boxed Set

Lightning Source UK Ltd.
Milton Keynes UK
UKHW010656211119
353971UK00001B/137/P